Books by
Joseph Xand

Dead Fall: A Zombie Novel (2nd Edition)
Dead Fall: Zero Day
Tomorrow Will Never Come

The Many Moons Saga:
Ganymede (Book One)

Coming Soon:
The Reaching
Callisto (Book Two of the Many Moons Saga)
Everything Charred and Smoldering (Short Stories)

Joseph Xand

Tomorrow Will Never Come

XANDLAND
XL
PRESS

Tyler, TX

Published by Xandland Press

Tomorrow Will Never Come and cover art, Copyright © Xandland Press, 2026

ISBN-13: 978-1-95-492930-2 (Paperback)

Library of Congress Control Number Pending

Printed in the United States

1 2 3 4 5 6 7 8 9 10 XP 33 32 31 30 29 28 27 26

For information regarding film or television rights,
please email Xandland Press at info@xandland.com

To see what else Xandland Press has to offer from Joseph Xand or other books,
visit Xandland.com

Contents

Prologue: The Hunt   1

Wakan   11

Uninvited Guests   21

Sheriff Dylan   33

The Hermit   40

Elden   45

Excuse the Mess   50

Town Meeting   55

The Devil of Black Hills   60

On the Run   70

Two Gods   74

The Rousey Family   81

Posse   90

Maggie   94

Preparations   100

The Deepest Scars   103

A Law Matter   111

Not Coming Back   115

Meeting with the Devil   119

Tomorrow Will Never Come   125

The Knife   139

Phoenix   142

One Hard Som' Bitch to Kill   145

Follow the Trail of Bodies   155

Epilogue: The Souls of Man   177

Prologue: The Hunt

THE SUN BAKED THE iron-bound prison wagon as it rattled through the godforsaken Badlands of South Dakota. Inside, the air was thick with the stench of sweat, blood, and despair. Only thin slivers of harsh light knifed through the narrow slits in the wooden walls, painting fleeting shadows on the figure chained to the floorboards.

Tall Foot sat hunched in the darkness. His wrists and ankles were raw from the iron manacles, chafing deeper with every jolt of the wagon. One eye was swollen shut, a purpled mess from the beatings he'd taken back in that stinking jailhouse. The other eye, sharp as a hawk's, burned with quiet fury. He was broad-shouldered and tall even when seated, his bronze skin marked with old scars and fresh bruises beneath the tattered remnants of his buckskin shirt.

The wagon lurched to a halt, wheels creaking in protest. Dust settled outside like a shroud. Tall Foot tugged at his chains, the metal biting into his flesh as he strained to peer through one of the slits. Through the narrow gap, he glimpsed towering pines in the far distance—a dark wall of forest promising freedom, or at least a fighting chance. Closer, booted feet thudded past, and he caught flashes of rough men: bearded faces, sweat-stained hats, holsters heavy with iron.

A key scraped and wrestled in the lock at the rear door. Tall Foot's heart pounded like war drums. He scooted back as far as the chains allowed, pressing his spine against the rough planks, every muscle coiled for whatever hell was coming.

The door swung open with a groan, and blinding sunlight flooded in, searing his good eye. He squinted against it, his battered form revealed at last: a proud Lakota warrior, stripped of his dignity, clothes ripped and bloodied from the fists and boots that had worked him over.

Framed in the doorway stood Prichard, a hard-bitten sonofabitch, his face etched with lines from too many years of whiskey, sun, and meanness. He didn't smile—couldn't, maybe, like the devil had carved it out of him long ago. He held the door wide with one callused hand, the other resting easy near the Colt on his hip.

Flanking him were two of his dogs: Curtis, a wiry bastard with a grin full of rotting teeth that made him look like a coyote sniffing carrion, and Willy, older and thicker, his eyes dull with the kind of cruelty that came from following orders without question.

Prichard jerked his chin toward the prisoner. Curtis and Willy clambered inside without a word, boots thudding on the wagon floor.

Tall Foot exploded into action the moment they reached for him. He kicked out savagely, his bare feet connecting with Curtis's shin, drawing a yelp. But chains hampered him, and they were on him like wolves—fists pounding into his ribs, his jaw, reopening cuts until blood trickled fresh down his chin. He fought like a cornered mountain lion, but it was no use. They pinned him, unlocked the manacles with grunts and curses, then hauled him toward the light.

Outside, the dry earth waited. Prichard stepped aside just as Curtis and Willy heaved Tall Foot from the wagon. He hit the ground hard, the impact jarring through his bones, dust billowing up around him like smoke from a gunshot. He rolled to his knees, gasping, tasting dirt.

A dozen men ringed him now—roughnecks, bounty hunters, and drifters, all armed to the teeth with Winchesters cradled in their arms and revolvers gleaming at their sides. They stared down at him with hungry eyes, some smirking, others chuckling low in their throats, sizing him up like a steer at auction. The forest loomed behind them, a distant green refuge under the vast, indifferent sky.

Tall Foot's gaze locked on Prichard, who stood chewing a splintered toothpick, his eyes cold as a snake's.

Prichard nodded once, then drew a long, wicked dagger from his belt. The blade was etched with Lakota markings—sacred patterns that twisted Tall Foot's gut. It had been his once, taken as a trophy.

With a casual flick, Prichard tossed it into the dirt at Tall Foot's feet. The knife thudded point-first, quivering.

"Pick it up," Prichard growled, voice like gravel under boot heels.

Tall Foot stared at the blade, then lifted his head to scan the circle of men. Grins widened. Hands tightened on rifle stocks, fingers itching near holstered pistols. He met Prichard's stare again and shook his head slow, defiant.

"Pick. It. Up."

The air thickened with tension. The men leaned in, eager, hands hovering like vultures over carrion.

Tall Foot shook his head once more.

Prichard glanced around, seeing the bloodlust in their eyes—the same hunger Tall Foot saw. He sighed, a sound heavy with mock exasperation.

"No one's gonna shoot you for pickin' up the knife."

Tall Foot held his gaze, unblinking.

Prichard turned to his crew. "You understand? No one shoots."

Grudging nods. Rifles lowered a fraction, postures eased, though the smirks lingered.

"Okay?" Prichard said to Tall Foot. "Pick it up."

Still, the warrior stared, silent as stone.

Prichard's patience snapped like a dry twig. "For fuck sakes."

He nodded to Curtis and Willy. They lunged forward, yanking Tall Foot to his feet with rough hands digging into his arms. Prichard scooped up the dagger himself and shoved it into Tall Foot's palm, forcing his bruised fingers to close around the bone handle.

Then they backed off, the circle widening.

Tall Foot looked down at the weapon in his grip, then at the ring of armed men, their faces alight with dark amusement. His eyes settled on Prichard.

Prichard pointed toward the distant trees. The men parted like a curtain, clearing the view to the shadowy woods.

"Go. Fast."

Confusion flickered across Tall Foot's battered features as he glanced at the forest, then back.

"Go. Into the woods. Now."

Tall Foot's brow furrowed. Prichard turned to his henchmen. "Does this one speak English?"

Curtis and Willy exchanged shrugs.

"Does he have any clue what I'm sayin'?"

More shrugs.

"Goddammit." Prichard raised his voice to the others. "Does anyone here speak Lakota so we can explain to this man—"

"What do you want?" Tall Foot cut in, his voice low and steady, English laced with the rhythm of his people's tongue.

The men shifted, surprised. Prichard turned slow, eyebrow cocked.

"I want you to run into those woods," he said. "And I want you to keep running. As fast as you can."

"Why?"

Prichard fished a tarnished pocket watch from his vest, flipping it open with a thumb. "Because I'm givin' you a ten-minute head start."

He snapped it shut. "Startin'...now."

Tall Foot's mouth parted, dawning horror widening his good eye. He scanned the circle again—grins returned, weapons gripped anew. The dagger felt suddenly heavy in his hand. Realization crashed over him like a stampede: this was no mercy. This was sport.

He opened his mouth, a protest rising—

"Nine minutes, forty-five seconds."

Panic surged. Tall Foot backed away, eyes darting. Then he spun and bolted toward the trees, legs pumping despite the ache in every muscle, bare feet pounding the parched earth.

The men erupted in hoots and hollers, jeering like demons at a hanging.

"Wooo! Look at that one run!" Curtis whooped, slapping Willy on the shoulder. "I told you this was a good one. I told you!"

"Yeah!" Curtis yelled after the fleeing figure. "You boys gonna git your money's worth today, boy howdy!"

Prichard watched impassive, toothpick working between his teeth as Tall Foot shrank toward the brush, a desperate shadow racing the coming storm.

"We'll see," he muttered, a faint, cold smile finally cracking his face.

***

The forest swallowed Tall Foot whole, a tangled maze of pine and scrub that clawed at his torn clothes and scraped his bare arms bloody. He ran hard, lungs burning, bare feet pounding over roots and rocks that tore at his soles. Every few strides he threw a glance over his shoulder, half-expecting to see the glint of rifle barrels already closing in. Sweat stung the cuts on his face; his swollen eye throbbed in time with his heartbeat. He leaped a fallen log, ducked beneath a low branch that whipped across his cheek, drawing fresh blood.

Gunshots cracked through the trees—sharp, deliberate pops that echoed off the trunks. Tall Foot skidded to a halt, chest heaving, ears straining. The shots weren't just behind him. They came from ahead, too, and from the sides. Voices followed—wild, drunken whoops and curses, the sound of men on horseback crashing through the underbrush. The hunt had begun in earnest, and they had him surrounded.

He veered sharply left, plunging deeper into the thicket, branches snapping against his shoulders like whips. The forest floor sloped unevenly; he stumbled once, caught himself on a tree trunk, and kept moving.

In another part of the woods, a knot of hunters spurred their mounts between the trees, yelling like coyotes on the scent. Rifles barked into the air, the muzzle flashes bright against the green shadows. Further off, another group picked their way down a steep incline, careful but eager, their horses snorting steam in the cool air. They fired too, shots ringing out in ragged volleys.

Tall Foot stopped beside a thick ponderosa pine, pressing his back to the rough bark, gulping air. Gunshots and shouts seemed to come from every direction now—behind, ahead, left, right. The men were closing the net. He looked down at the dagger still clutched in his fist, its blade streaked with dirt and his own blood. Fear tightened his throat. He shoved the knife into his belt, turned, and ran again.

The hunters reined in their horses, milling in a small clearing. One of them—a lean man with a patchy beard—squinted at the ground.

"I think I got a trail," he said, pointing. "Footprints, headed north."

He waved the others over. They gathered, studied the tracks, then spurred off in that direction, horses kicking up pine needles.

Moments later, Tall Foot leaned against another tree, breath rasping in his throat. He eased his head around the trunk, peering through the branches. Below him, in a narrow gulley, five riders moved slowly on horseback. One lagged behind the rest, cursing under his breath.

"Come on, you big whore," the lagging hunter growled, slapping his legs against the horse's flanks. "You act like you ain't never been in the woods before."

Tall Foot watched the man, then tilted his head back to study the branches above him. He scanned the ground, spotted a palm-sized rock half-buried in the needles, and scooped it up.

The lagging hunter heard a rustle in the bushes ahead. He turned, saw the branches shake, and grinned crookedly.

"Let's just see who nabs him first this time," he muttered. He called softly to the others ahead, but they had already vanished between the trees. Shrugging, he guided his horse toward the sound, rifle raised.

Tall Foot crouched low on a thick branch overhead, muscles coiled. As the hunter passed beneath, he dropped.

The impact was brutal. Both men crashed to the ground in a tangle of limbs and dust. The hunter's rifle flew from his hands, skittering across the needles. He groaned, rolling onto his back, pain twisting his face. Tall Foot loomed over him, knife raised high, blade glinting.

The hunter's eyes widened, terror draining the color from his face. He threw his hands up.

"Please! I've got children!"

Tall Foot hesitated, knife trembling an inch above the man's chest.

A gunshot cracked. Bark exploded from the tree beside Tall Foot's head. He spun to see the other four hunters charging through the gulley, rifles leveled.

In one fluid motion, Tall Foot hurled the dagger. It struck true, burying to the hilt in the shoulder of the nearest rider. The man screamed and toppled from his saddle.

Another bullet whined past. Tall Foot scooped the fallen rifle from the dirt, vaulted onto the lagging hunter's horse, and kicked it into a gallop. The animal surged forward, hooves thundering.

The hunters roared past the lagging man, who staggered to his feet, clutching his arm.

"That damn savage stole my horse and gun!" he bellowed. "Go git that sumbitch!"

Bullets snapped through the air. Tall Foot hunched low, teeth clenched. A hot line of pain seared across his side; blood soaked his shirt and ran warm down his leg. He glanced right—more riders bursting from the trees.

"There he is, boys!" one shouted. "He done got one of our horses!"

Tall Foot yanked the reins, veering left toward a fallen pine. Bullets hammered into the horse's flank. The animal screamed, legs buckling as it tried to leap the log. It stumbled, pitching forward.

Tall Foot flew from the saddle, slamming shoulder-first into a tree trunk. The world tilted. He crumpled to the ground, dazed, tasting blood.

His right leg lay twisted at a sick angle, white bone jutting through torn flesh and blood-soaked cloth. Pain roared through him, white-hot. He reached for the rifle, fingers scraping dirt, but it lay yards away. His body refused to move.

Boots crunched closer. The hunters dismounted, circling him slowly, rifles loose in their hands.

One laughed low. "Gut shot's mine."

"Hell it is," another snarled. "That'un's from my gun."

"Well, I know that shot in the leg was from me."

"Oh? So the rest of us just hit horse?"

The lead hunter swung his Winchester off his shoulder and leveled it at Tall Foot's face. The barrel hovered inches from his forehead.

Tall Foot stared up through the haze of pain, breath shallow, blood pooling beneath him.

"Won't be no doubt 'bout this one," the hunter said.

The horses shied at the muzzle flash. The rifle roared.

Wakan

THE WIND SWEPT COLD and sharp across the vast South
Dakota prairie, carrying the bite of late winter under a
steel-gray sky. Snow lingered in patchy drifts along the shadows
of rocky hills, and the ground was a mix of frozen earth and mud
churned by wagon wheels. Wakan, a Lakota girl of twelve winters,
rode steady down a worn trail on a sturdy mare, her small frame
bundled in thick traditional garb: a heavy wool dress over leggings,
fur-lined moccasins, and a buffalo-hide coat that swallowed her
slight build. A modest headdress of eagle feathers crowned her
braided hair, fluttering faintly in the breeze. The horse—packed
high with rolled blankets, bundled furs, and saddlebags bulging
with trade goods—moved with calm purpose beneath her.

She guided the mare through open wilderness: sweeping fields
of brown grass rippling like waves, stands of bare cottonwood
along frozen creeks, and jagged outcrops of rock that jutted from
the earth like old bones.

The trail dipped into a broad valley, flanked on one side by
a rough-split rail fence half-buried in snow. Beyond it stretched
more open plain; on the other rose dense forests of pine climbing

steep, shadowed hills. Wakan's dark eyes scanned the horizon, ever watchful.

Something moved at the edge of the treeline. She reined in gently, gaze narrowing. A lone man emerged from the shadows—a towering figure draped in a massive bear-skin jacket, the fur matted and dark with old blood and weather. A deep hood shadowed his face, and a thick scarf covered his mouth and nose, leaving only a strip of skin and piercing eyes visible. He hefted the gutted carcass of a huge wild boar onto his broad shoulders with a grunt, the animal's tusks gleaming dull in the weak light, blood still dripping from its slashed throat.

Wakan watched, still as stone, as the Bear Man started into the trees. Then, as if sensing her stare, he paused and turned. Those eyes—cold, unreadable—locked with hers across the distance. The wind howled between them. Neither moved for a long moment. At last, Wakan dropped her gaze first, a flicker of unease tightening her grip on the reins.

The Bear Man turned away without a sound and vanished into the dark wall of pines, swallowed by the forest as though he'd never been.

Later, as the sun bled low toward the horizon, Wakan trotted the mare toward a distant log cabin nestled in a wide, windswept field. Thin smoke curled from the stone chimney, carrying the faint scent of burning pine. A sturdy barn stood nearby, its doors weathered gray, and beyond the homestead the wilderness pressed close—endless hills rolling into the darkening sky.

At the cabin, Audrey Josephs, a hardy woman with wind-chapped cheeks and auburn hair tied back in a practical knot, pinned fresh-washed laundry to a sagging line. Steam rose from the basket at her feet. She lifted a heavy sheet, shaking it out, when movement on the path caught her eye. Wakan approached at an easy trot.

"Paul?" Audrey called, voice carrying over the wind.

Her husband, the local chaplain who served both settler and reservation alike, paused mid-swing, his axe hovering over a thick log on the chopping block. Sweat glistened on his brow despite the cold. He straightened, wiped his sleeve across his face, and followed Audrey's gaze.

Wakan drew nearer, the mare's hooves thudding softly on the frozen ground. Paul's eyes widened. He glanced back at Audrey, who answered with a helpless shrug and a slow shake of her head.

Paul leaned the axe against the block and strode toward the split-rail gate. Audrey let the sheet fall back into the basket and hurried after him.

They met Wakan just as she guided the horse through the gate.

"Wakan?" Paul said, voice thick with surprise and concern. "What on earth are you doing here?"

Wakan spoke clear English, her words shaped by the soft cadence of the Lakota tongue.

"My father wanted me to bring Itháṅčhaṅ to you."

"Itháṅčhaṅ?"

She reached forward and patted the mare's strong neck.

"It means 'strong heart.' I hope you don't mind."

Paul stepped closer, studying the horse with open astonishment.

"My God...is this the same mare I bought off the Wellington place last year?"

He moved to the animal's flank, brushing aside the thick winter coat to reveal the branded mark: a simple circle with a bold "W" at its center.

"Last time I laid eyes on her," Paul muttered, "I couldn't get within twenty feet without her trying to stove my head in."

He offered a hand to help Wakan down. She swung off gracefully as she spoke.

"Father told you I could tame any beast. It is only a matter of listening."

She began loosening the rawhide straps on the packed bags.

"But my father says I am old enough now for a steed of my own. He sent me with offerings of trade for Ithánčhan, if you are willing to part with her."

Audrey drew nearer, worry creasing her brow as Wakan continued pulling items from the bags—thick wool blankets dyed in rich earth tones, soft beaver and fox furs, a pouch of fragrant pipe tobacco. Audrey's eyes flicked to Paul, wide and troubled.

"I have brought several blankets," Wakan went on, laying them carefully on the frozen ground. "Some fine furs. Some of the tobacco you favor—"

"Wakan," Audrey interrupted gently, "did you ride all this way alone? It's three hard days from the reservation."

Wakan nodded, chin lifted with quiet pride.

"My father says I am as capable as any warrior of our people. He believes this journey—this trade—will prove it."

Audrey and Paul exchanged a long, heavy look, the wind tugging at their clothes.

"So, as I was saying," Wakan continued, "there is plenty here for you to choose from. Or I can bring more if it pleases you. But if you wish to keep Ithánčhan for yourselves, I will understand. She is a good horse and will serve—"

"Okay, okay," Paul cut in, raising a hand. "We'll work something out for...Ithánčhan. You've clearly put the work in."

A bright, genuine smile broke across Wakan's face, lighting her young features.

"Well, I'll unload these bags so you can see everything properly," she said, reaching for another strap, "but I should start for home before dark—"

Audrey stepped forward quickly.

"Paul..."

He nodded, understanding at once.

"Absolutely not, young lady," Paul said firmly. "You'll stay for supper and the night. No sense starting back this late."

"But—"

"I've got to ride to the capital myself in the morning," Paul went on. "Your reservation's only a little out of my way. I'll see you home safe."

Wakan hesitated, uncertainty flickering across her face.

Paul softened his tone. "Sorry, little one. That's the condition of any trade for Ithánčhan. We leave at first light."

After a moment, Wakan relented with a small nod.

"Okay, then," Paul said. "Why don't you see that Ithánčhan gets watered and a good feed of oats. Bed her down in the barn. Audrey's about to start supper."

Wakan gathered the reins and led the mare toward the barn, her steps light despite the long ride.

Audrey and Paul watched her go. Audrey's face was tight with worry. Paul slipped an arm around her waist and pulled her close.

"I know," he murmured.

Together they turned and walked back toward the cabin, the door creaking open to the promise of warmth as twilight settled cold and deep over the prairie.

***

The fire in the hearth crackled low, throwing flickering orange light across the rough-hewn logs of the Josephs' cabin. Outside, the South Dakota night pressed cold against the walls, wind moaning through the cracks like a restless spirit. Inside, the air smelled of pine smoke, stewed rabbit, and the faint lye scent of fresh-washed linens.

Audrey knelt beside the makeshift cot in the corner—a thick pallet of straw topped with quilts and one of the soft beaver furs Wakan had brought. She tucked the heavy blankets snug around the girl's shoulders, smoothing a stray braid from her forehead.

"There now," Audrey murmured, her voice soft as lamplight. "Isn't this better than sleeping on the cold ground?"

Wakan's dark eyes gleamed in the fire glow. "It wasn't so bad. It rained some last night, but it didn't last long."

Audrey pulled the covers higher, tucking them tight beneath Wakan's chin. "Lord have mercy. You're lucky you didn't catch your death out there."

Wakan fell quiet for a moment, staring at the shadowed rafters overhead. Then, in a small voice: "I saw that man today. Not too far from here."

Audrey tilted her head, curious. "What man is that, sweetheart?"

"The Bear Man."

Audrey's brow lifted. "Bear Man?"

From across the room, Paul stood at the small bookshelf built into the wall, running a callused finger along the spines of his few precious volumes—mostly scripture, a worn almanac, and a couple of dog-eared novels traded from passing wagon trains.

"She must mean that old hermit," he said without turning. "Lives up north of the Reynolds' dairy. The one always wrapped in that big bearskin coat."

Audrey nodded slowly. "Ahh."

But Wakan shook her head, braids brushing the quilt.

"I've heard some of the settler children talk about him before," she said. "They say that's not a coat. They say he is an evil bear spirit."

Paul selected a slim leather-bound book, a faint smile tugging at his beard as he crossed the puncheon floor toward the cot.

"Is that so?" he asked, voice warm with amusement.

Wakan nodded solemnly. "Uh-huh. They say he eats children."

Audrey and Paul both chuckled, the sound low and gentle in the quiet cabin.

"Oh, honey," Audrey said, leaning closer. "That's just a tale parents tell to keep little ones from wandering off. 'If you don't mind your chores and stay close to home, the Bear Man will come in the night and gobble you up!'"

She growled playfully, pretending to snap at Wakan's neck with chomping teeth while tickling her ribs. Wakan squealed and squirmed, laughter bubbling out despite herself.

"But it's not real," Audrey finished, smoothing the girl's hair once more.

"You promise?" Wakan asked, eyes wide.

"I do," Audrey said firmly.

Paul settled onto the edge of a nearby stool. "That fellow—the Bear Man, as you call him—he's just a harmless old mountain man who keeps to himself out in the wild. Lives alone, traps his meat, trade his furs, doesn't bother a soul. That's all there is to it."

Wakan offered a small, relieved smile and sank deeper into the warm nest of blankets, her eyelids already growing heavy.

Audrey brushed a final strand of hair from the girl's face. "Now get some rest, young lady. You've got a long ride home tomorrow."

Wakan answered with a wide, sleepy yawn. Audrey leaned down and pressed a tender kiss to her forehead.

Through Wakan's drowsy eyes the room tilted sideways. The firelight blurred and sharpened as her lids fluttered.

Audrey and Paul rose and moved toward the two rocking chairs near the hearth. Their voices dropped to hushed murmurs, but in the small cabin the words still carried, soft and urgent, to the cot in the corner.

"My God, Paul..."

"I know, honey."

"She was out there all alone..."

Paul rested a steady hand on Audrey's shoulder as they reached the chairs and sat.

"She's safe now."

"She could have been killed," Audrey whispered, voice trembling. "If those men had found her—"

"But she wasn't," Paul said quietly. "And they didn't."

He leaned back, opened his book, and slid his spectacles onto his nose. The fire popped, sending sparks up the chimney.

Audrey perched on the edge of her chair, glancing back toward the darkened corner where Wakan lay.

"Once we reach the reservation," Paul continued, "I'll speak with her father. Make sure he understands what's happening out here."

Audrey's fingers worried the hem of her apron. "He should have known already. Perhaps we shouldn't have waited so long."

Paul drew a slow, heavy breath. He turned a page without reading it.

"Perhaps not."

The wind rattled the shutters again. In the cot, Wakan's breathing deepened into the steady rhythm of sleep as the fire settled into glowing embers and the vast, frozen night closed tighter around the little cabin on the prairie.

Uninvited Guests

WAKAN'S EYES SNAPPED OPEN. Audrey's face loomed close, pale and urgent in the faint glow, her hand shaking the girl's shoulder.

"Wakan? Wakan, honey? I need you to wake up right now."

Wakan's voice came thick with sleep. "Huh?"

In the deeper shadows near the front window, Paul stood rigid, peering through a crack in the shutters. A double-barreled shotgun gripped tight in his hands.

"They're coming up the front path," he said low and hard. "We need to get her out of here."

He crossed the room in quick strides.

Wakan pushed up on her elbows, heart already pounding. "What's going on?"

Paul snatched her small rucksack from beside the cot while Audrey pulled the quilts away.

"You're gonna have to leave out the back door, okay," Audrey said, voice trembling but steady. "Straight out into the woods."

"But..." Wakan looked to Paul, confusion sharp in her eyes. "I thought I was leaving with you."

"I thought you were too, Wakan," Paul said grimly, "but not now. And I don't have time to explain."

He tossed the rucksack at the foot of the cot, then gripped her under one arm and hauled her upright—rougher than he'd ever touched her before.

"Paul!" Audrey protested.

"Gather up her things," he snapped. "Quickly, now!"

Audrey sprang into motion, stuffing Wakan's few belongings into the pack—moccasins, the small headdress, a pouch of pemmican.

Paul dropped to one knee in front of the girl, his callused hand gentle now against the side of her head.

"I'm sorry," he said, voice cracking just a little, "but this is how it has to be, okay? You know your way home. I need you to get there as fast as you can."

"But—"

"We'll be fine."

Audrey handed Paul the packed rucksack, then sat beside Wakan on the cot's edge.

"You'll do just as Miss Audrey told you," Paul went on. "Out the back and straight to the woods. Then you'll keep going until you're home."

"On foot?" Wakan's voice was small. "What about Itháṅčhaṅ?"

"You can't get her right now," Audrey said softly. "I'm sorry."

"But she's yours," Paul added quickly. "We'll take good care of her until you get back."

Audrey's head snapped toward him, eyes sharp with disbelief. Paul refused to meet her gaze, keeping his focus on Wakan. But the girl saw it too—the lie plain on his face.

Outside, a horse neighed loud and nervous. Hooves thudded on frozen ground—many of them.

"Now repeat what we told you," Paul said.

Wakan tried to peer past him toward the front door. He gave her shoulders a urgent shake.

"Wakan!"

"Out the back," she recited, voice quavering. "Straight to the woods. Don't stop."

"That's right. Not for anything."

Paul drew a deep, steadying breath. Together he and Audrey hustled her across the puncheon floor to the back door. They pressed close as Paul eased it open a crack, shotgun ready, scanning the black wall of trees beyond. Cold air rushed in, carrying the distant smell of horse sweat.

Suddenly, he dug into his shirt pocket and pulled out a small bundle of folded papers, edges worn and creased. He stared at them a heartbeat, then pressed them into Wakan's hands.

"Give these to your father," he whispered fiercely. "He'll know what to do with them. No one else but him."

Audrey's eyes went wide. "Paul, no!"

He ignored her, holding Wakan's gaze.

Tears glistened in Audrey's eyes. She dropped to her knees and wrapped the girl in a crushing hug, arms trembling.

Paul touched Audrey's shoulder. "You should go, too."

She stood, shaking her head hard. "I'm staying."

"Audrey—"

"If I'm not here, they'll know I fled. They'll come straight to the woods looking for me. If I stay…Wakan has a shot."

Paul looked at her long and hard, then nodded once.

Laughter—rough, drunken, cruel—drifted from the front of the cabin.

Paul glanced toward the sound, then back. "She has to go. Now."

Audrey nodded. Paul pushed Wakan gently but firmly through the door. He leaned close, breath warm against her ear as she stared into the swallowing darkness of the forest.

"Stick to the woods. Stay off the roads and trails."

Wakan nodded, clutching the papers tight.

"Hey there, Reverend!" a voice bellowed from the front. "Won't you come on out here so we can talk!"

Audrey and Paul exchanged one last look. Paul shoved Wakan fully outside.

"Run. Now."

The door shut with a soft but final thud.

"Don't make us come in there after you, now!" the voice taunted again.

Wakan turned toward the dark treeline and bolted, small legs pumping as she crashed through the underbrush.

At the front of the cabin, Curtis—teeth rotten from chew—stood among a knot of mounted men, torches flickering in their fists, casting orange light over hard, dirty faces. Rifles and sidearms glinted at every hip.

Beside him Prichard was old hate. He was the boss, and every man there knew it. Curtis was his right hand. The rest—Willie, Bobby, Reilly, Sneed, and Giles—were a ragged pack of killers, beards matted, clothes stained with trail dust and worse.

"Why don't you and your pretty little wife come out and talk to us civil-like!" Curtis called, grinning wide.

Prichard reached over and tugged Giles's torch lower, lighting the cigarette clenched in his teeth. Then he turned to Curtis and spat into the dirt.

"Go around back," he said low. "Make sure they ain't tryin' to head for the woods."

Curtis scowled. "Why can't one of them do it?"

Prichard took a long drag, eyes never leaving the cabin door. "'Cause I told you to do it."

Curtis muttered under his breath and swung down, heading around the side.

"Come on out here now, Reverend!" Prichard shouted. "Don't make me smoke you out!"

He glanced at the barn, then nodded to Giles. Giles dismounted and jogged that direction, torch held high.

In the woods near the cabin, Wakan pushed through tangled brush, breath coming in sharp gasps. She glanced back—just in time to see Curtis round the corner, revolver drawn, scanning the darkness.

She dropped low, heart hammering, and crept along the treeline until she could see the front yard again.

Curtis crept to a side window and peered in.

Through the glass he saw Paul and Audrey near the front door. Paul's hand rested briefly on his wife's shoulders, then moved to the knob.

"I ain't one for askin' twice," Prichard warned. "But I'm feelin' generous. So I'm givin' you one more chance! Come out here now, and I won't—"

The door creaked open.

Prichard's men tensed, weapons rising.

Paul stepped out slow, rifle in hand but palms raised. He pulled the door nearly shut behind him.

As he descended the porch steps, the circle of riders tightened.

"I'm not sure what all this is about, Prichard," Paul said evenly, "but you needn't have brought all your friends. You know I'm a man of peace."

"Then you won't be needin' that," Prichard replied.

He nodded to Willie, who snatched the rifle away.

"Now. Where's that pretty little wife o' yours?"

"Whatever business you think you have here, she's not involved."

"Oh, I doubt that, Reverend. Somethin' tells me she's ever' bit as involved as you." A beat. "Now get her out here."

Paul shook his head.

The door burst open behind him. Curtis shoved Audrey forward. She stumbled down the steps, catching the rail at the last moment.

"Audrey!" Paul started toward her.

Willie's rifle butt cracked across his jaw. Paul dropped hard into the frozen dirt.

From the woods, Wakan stifled a gasp.

Audrey rushed to her husband's side. "Paul!"

She helped him to his knees. Blood trickled from a split cheek.

Prichard smirked. "Willie! Is that any way to treat a man of the cloth?" he asked as he dismounted.

His men laughed, low and ugly.

"Rumor has it, Preacher-man," Prichard went on, pacing, hand resting on his holstered Colt, "that you got a mind to head up to the capital this week. That you got an appointment with the Injun Affairs people."

Paul wiped blood from his mouth. "I have no idea what you're talking about."

Prichard stopped. "Uh-huh. I also heard you had some evidence you was plannin' to turn over. Evidence that points to certain...goings-on. But I'm guessin' you don't know nothin' about that neither."

Paul said nothing.

Prichard turned to Reilly and Sneed. "Toss the cabin. Every inch."

The two men bolted inside. Glass shattered almost immediately; furniture crashed.

Giles jogged back from the barn. "Ain't nobody in the barn, but there's a horse that ain't with the others. Looks like it was rode hard today."

Prichard's gaze drilled into Paul.

Paul hesitated as more destruction echoed from inside. "I bought that horse off the Wellington place a while back. Wasn't tamed yet. They delivered her today."

Prichard looked at Giles. Giles shrugged. "Got the Wellington brand."

Prichard nodded slowly. "Now. About that evidence."

"I already told you—"

"I've been told this evidence don't just name me and mine," Prichard cut in. "It's got a list of clients, too. Powerful men gettin' nervous."

He crouched close, adjusting his hat brim.

"So why don't you tell me where it is, and we can ease some minds."

"I don't have what you're looking for."

Prichard stared a long moment. Then rose. In one smooth motion he drew his revolver and fired into Audrey's thigh.

Her scream tore through the night, just enough to blur out Wakan's own.

Paul lunged. "AUDREY!"

Willie and Bobby pinned him down.

Audrey writhed, blood soaking her skirt dark.

Reilly appeared in the doorway. "We ain't found nothin'."

Prichard's voice rose to a roar. "What about it now, Preacher-man? Where's the evidence?"

Paul stared at his wife, tears cutting tracks through the dirt on his face.

Prichard cocked the hammer again.

"Okay!" Paul shouted.

Silence fell.

"Okay," he repeated quieter. He met Audrey's pleading eyes, then looked away. "I was goin' to the capital. To meet with the Bureau of Indian Affairs."

Audrey shook her head almost imperceptibly.

"But I wasn't turning over evidence," Paul continued. "Just goin' to tell them what I know. What I *think* I know. All the evidence...I never wrote it down. Didn't want anyone to find it." He tapped his temple. "It's all up here."

A heavy quiet settled.

Prichard nodded once. Willie tossed him Paul's rifle. Prichard caught it, worked the action.

"I've always thought the worst insult one man can give another is to kill him with his own gun," he said. "That's why I make a point of it."

He raised the rifle and fired.

Paul's head snapped back. His body collapsed limp.

In the woods, Wakan stood, both hands clamped tight against her mouth as tears welled in her eyes.

"NO!" Audrey screamed.

She dragged herself across the dirt to him, cradling his ruined head, rocking and sobbing.

Behind the men, in the distant flicker of torchlight, she spotted Wakan standing frozen among the bushes. Their eyes locked. Audrey shook her head fiercely—*no, child!*

Wakan dropped back into the shadows, tears streaming.

Prichard turned to Willie and Bobby. "Torch the place."

The two men hurried inside. Moments later, flames licked up the doorway and windows, orange light blooming across the yard.

"You won't get away with this, Prichard," Audrey spat through tears and pain.

He looked down at her.

"You'll hang," she said. "All of you will hang."

Prichard almost smiled. Almost like he knew how. "That may be, Miss Josephs. But we ain't hangin' tonight."

He leveled the pistol.

From the woods, Wakan watched the muzzle flash. Audrey slumped beside her husband.

Wakan buried her face in her hands, shoulders shaking with silent sobs.

She lifted her head. Prichard was scanning the treeline, eyes narrowed—he sensed something.

He turned to Curtis, Reilly, and Giles. "Check the woods. Make sure these two was alone."

Curtis groaned. "Why do I always get the bullshit work?"

Prichard sighed. "We've known each other a long time, Curtis, and I think of you like a brother. But I ain't one for repeatin' myself."

Curtis muttered and waved the others toward the trees.

Over Prichard's shoulder, young Sneed—the scrawniest of the bunch—lifted a foot to his stirrup.

"Sneed," Prichard said without looking.

Sneed froze. "Sir."

"Come here."

Sneed approached, eyes flicking to the bodies.

"Are you goin' somewhere?"

Sneed swallowed. "I just...I seen him preach once."

Prichard glanced at Paul's corpse. "Well...you won't be seein' him preach anymore." A beat. "Now why were you gettin' on the horse?"

"I was...ain't we goin' to get that hermit?"

Flames roared higher behind them, bathing the yard in hellish light.

"We went over it several times," Prichard said patiently. "People will come when they see the fire. Send someone to get the sheriff. Let the *sheriff* send you to get the hermit."

Sneed nodded quickly. "Okay. Yeah. That's right."

"There's a process and an order to things," Prichard said. "Get things out of order, and it all goes to shit."

Sneed nodded again. Then: "Think I can have his coat?"

Prichard blinked. "What?"

"His bear coat. I really like it."

Prichard shrugged. "Sure. Whatever."

Sneed brightened. "Hey...Prichard?"

"Yeah?"

"You think it'll itch? The coat, I mean?"

Prichard mounted his white horse. "You know what's itchy? A rope around the neck. Stay focused. I'm goin' to update the bossman."

Behind them, Curtis, Reilly, and Giles reached the treeline, torches hissing as they pushed into the brush.

Prichard spurred his horse and rode off into the night.

From deep in the shadows, Wakan watched him go. Then, clutching the folded papers tight against her chest, she turned and slipped silently deeper into the dark woods.

Sheriff Dylan

A SHARP KNOCK RATTLED the cabin door, cutting through the stillness of the night.

Outside, Sheriff Dylan's place stood alone on a rise of scrub pine and frozen grass, a low log structure with a sagging porch and a single lantern glowing in the front window. The door creaked open. Sheriff Dylan—fifties, grizzled, shoulders heavy from years of carrying a badge and a grudge—peered out into the dark.

Wakan stood on the stoop, small and shivering, hair tangled with twigs, face streaked with dirt and tears. Her rucksack hung off one shoulder; the folded papers were tucked safe inside her coat.

Dylan's eyes flicked over her, then scanned the yard, searching the shadows of the trees.

"Yeah?" he grunted. "What do you want?"

"Are you the sheriff?"

"Yeah." He stepped outside, pulling the door shut behind him with a soft thud. "What you doin' out this late?"

Wakan's words tumbled out in a rush. "My friends were killed by this group of guys and I saw the whole thing and I was told to go straight home and tell my father but I think I need to let a lawman know, since they were murdered—"

"Whoa, whoa, now. Slow down." Dylan raised a hand. "Who was murdered?"

"Pastor Josephs and Miss Audrey. That's his wife. I was visiting them, staying the night, when he gave me some papers and told me to go hide in the woods. And then these men told them—"

"Papers? What papers?"

"I don't know. I haven't looked at 'em yet. But I think the people who killed Pastor Josephs wanted them."

"So these men...they wanted the papers, so they killed Paul and Audrey?"

Wakan nodded, breath fogging in the cold.

"And where are these papers now?"

The question stopped her cold. She hesitated. "They're...in the woods. I hid them in a hole in a hollow tree. I wasn't sure who I could trust."

Dylan's mouth twitched. "That's good thinkin'. Good thinkin'." He studied her a moment. "And you know where to find this tree and these papers? You can bring me to 'em?"

Wakan stared back, then nodded slowly.

"Good. Good." He leaned closer. "Now, Paul and his wife are dead? What can you tell me about the men who killed 'em?"

Wakan thought. "There was six...no, seven of them. But...I think they're going to go after the hermit next."

"Hermit?"

"Yeah. The one who wears the bear-skin coat." She swallowed. "I think they're going to tell you that *he* killed them."

Dylan's jaw worked. "Okay. What else about these men? Did you get a good look at 'em? Could you identify 'em?"

Wakan nodded firmly.

"You sure? It's dark out."

"All the men had torches. The yard was lit up like daylight."

Dylan nodded again, slow and thoughtful. "I see. Good...good."

A horse neighed sharp and close. Both of them turned toward the tree-lined drive. Hooves pounded fast, coming hard.

"Did someone follow you here?" Dylan asked, voice dropping low.

Wakan's eyes went wide. "I came through the woods."

Dylan's hand clamped around her arm—hard—and he yanked her toward a small shed beside the cabin. He fumbled with the latch, pulled the door open.

"I want you to hide in here until I find out who this is."

Wakan hesitated.

"Go on, now."

She stepped inside. The shed smelled of damp earth and old tools—shovels, hoes, a rusted scythe leaned against the wall. Dylan shut the door behind her. The latch clicked.

Wakan pressed her face to a crack between the slats. The horse was closer now, hooves slowing to a stop.

"Sheriff! Thank God you're up!" a young voice called.

"Hell, Harry! I could hear you barrelin' this way from about a mile back! What the hell you doin' here this time o' night?"

Wakan squinted through the gap. A boy—maybe fifteen, lanky and wild-eyed—sat astride a sweating horse.

"Out at the Josephs' farm! They're dead, Sheriff! Pastor Paul and Miss Audrey are dead! My daddy sent me to get you!"

Dylan jogged over. "Dead! What! How?"

Inside the shed, Wakan's mouth went dry. Hadn't she already told him that? Why was he acting surprised? Was it to protect her?

"Somebody up an' kilt 'em! That's what my daddy said! And one guy there told my daddy it was that old hermit, lives up in the hills!"

"Hermit? Harry, has your daddy been hittin' the moonshine again?"

Dylan lifted his lantern, the light falling across the boy's face.

"No! Well...yeah, but he's sober, I swear! He went to check on the Josephs on account of the fire—"

"Fire?"

"Yep! That hermit torched the place!" Harry pointed back the way he'd come. "Go git whatever you need, and I'll ride back with you."

Dylan paused, thinking. "No. Harry, you head into town fast as you can. Round up some men to help with the fire." He paused. "I'll head over there now."

Harry hesitated.

"Go on! Before that fire spreads an' burns down half the county!"

Harry wheeled his horse around and galloped off into the dark.

Dylan stood watching him go. Then he turned his head slowly toward the shed.

Wakan's breath caught as their eyes seemed to meet through the slats. Dylan started up the porch steps.

The cabin door opened and shut behind him.

Wakan pressed her ear to the wood. She heard the faint whinny of a horse—then saw, through the back crack, Prichard's white horse tied to a post behind the cabin.

She shoved at the door. It didn't budge.

Her gaze darted around the cramped space: a hoe leaning against the wall, the dirt floor under the back wall. She grabbed the hoe, drove it into the earth, and began to dig.

Inside the cabin, Dylan shut the front door and leaned against it, palm flat on the wood. He set the lantern on a side table, then crossed to the back room.

Prichard sat at the table, boots up, cigarette glowing in the dim.

"That somebody about the fire?" he asked.

Dylan rounded the table, snatching his gun belt off a cabinet and buckling it on with angry jerks.

"You mean the fire ain't nobody told you to start? Yeah. Along with some Injun girl."

Prichard's eyes narrowed. "What Injun girl?"

"The very one who watched you kill the pastor and his wife. The same one who has the evidence we were lookin' for."

Prichard stood. "Where is she?"

"Relax. She's locked up in the shed."

"What are we gonna do?"

Dylan shook his head. "We stick to the plan. I'll head out to the Josephs, then send a posse out for the hermit. I want them draggin' his body through the middle of town by first light." He met Prichard's gaze. "You see to the girl. She says she hid the evidence near the Josephs' cabin. Have her bring you to it. Do whatever you have to do. Get your hands on it, then get rid of her."

Prichard's mouth twitched. "An Injun girl could be worth money."

Dylan's glare was cold steel. "She's a liability. And we could all be swingin' from trees with what she knows. Get rid of her."

Prichard nodded once. Dylan grabbed his hat off the wall and stormed out, slamming the door behind him.

***

Outside, Prichard pulled the cabin door shut. He walked to the shed, lantern in one hand, sidearm already drawn in the other. He unlatched the door, yanked it open, and raised the light.

The shed was empty.

He leaned in, sweeping the beam across the tools and dirt. His eyes landed on the small hole dug under the back wall, the hoe lying beside it, fresh earth scattered like blood.

"Shit."

***

In the woods beyond, Wakan ran—small feet flying over frozen ground, branches whipping her face, breath coming in sharp, ragged bursts. She threw frantic glances over her shoulder, the lantern light fading behind her as she plunged deeper into the dark.

The Hermit

T HE SUN HAD CLIMBED just high enough to burn off the morning frost. A dilapidated cabin squatted low among the pines, half-buried in snowdrifts and fallen needles, its weathered logs patched with moss and mud. Furs—bear, elk, wolf—hung limp from a sagging porch rail, tanning in the weak winter light. An axe blade was buried deep in a bloodstained stump near the porch, the handle still glistening with fresh sap.

THWOP! The sharp sound of steel splitting bone and wood echoed from inside.

On the front door, the metal cans and tin plates strung together on twine rattled faintly, as though the cabin itself had taken a breath.

Inside, a skinned deer carcass lay sprawled across a rough-hewn table, blood dripping steadily onto the dirt floor. THWOP! A cleaver came down hard, shearing off a thick slab of meat. The man wielding it stood with his back to the room, massive in his bearskin coat. THWOP! Another strike. He reached into the cavity, fingers digging deep, and yanked a fistful of guts free, tossing them into a rusted metal bowl at his feet with a wet slap.

He raised the cleaver again—then froze. The cans rattled louder. He hurled the cleaver. It thunked deep into the table, quivering.

***

In the woods beyond the cabin, Wakan stumbled forward, breath clouding in the cold air. Her foot caught on a low-running vine; she yanked it free with a grunt and kept moving, eyes darting through the trees.

"Hello?" she called, voice small but steady. "Mr. Bear Man?"

She turned in a slow circle, scanning the shadows. "Hello? I don't mean to bother you. I just want to talk."

A rustle in the brush made her spin. A flock of ravens exploded upward, black wings beating the air. Wakan flinched, then quickened her pace.

A twig snapped behind her. She whirled—caught a flicker of movement in the deep shade, gone before she could focus. Heart hammering, she veered the other way, jumping a fallen pine and ducking under a low branch. Brambles clawed at her legs; she plunged through, arms shielding her face, thorns tearing at her sleeves.

She burst out the other side and stopped, chest heaving, hands on her knees.

Her eyes landed on a thick patch of bushes. Something watched her from within.

The bushes erupted. A shape lunged—hands appeared, swift and sure, yanking a burlap sack over her head. Darkness swallowed her.

***

When she opened her eyes again, she saw the world through a tear in the coarse fabric. She lay on a filthy pallet of hides and old blankets, the smell of woodsmoke and old blood thick in her nose. Her left wrist was chained to the bedframe; she tugged. The iron held fast.

A door creaked open behind her. Heavy footsteps crossed the floor. The Bear Man entered, arms full of split wood. He moved to the cast-iron stove, opened the door, and crouched to feed the fire, his broad back to her.

"Are you gonna eat me?" Wakan asked, voice small.

He turned his head slightly, then dropped the wood with a clatter and crossed to her in two strides. She tried to shrink away, but the chain stopped her. He grabbed the sack and ripped it off.

They stared at each other. He was older than she'd expected—late forties, perhaps—face weathered to leather, full beard streaked with gray, eyes sharp and unreadable beneath heavy brows. The bearskin coat hung open over a stained flannel shirt.

"You're a bit scrawny for my taste," he said, voice low and rough. He tossed the sack aside. "But I suppose you'd do in a pinch."

He turned back to the stove and crouched again, shoving more wood into the flames.

"What do you want with me?" Wakan asked.

"Kid, you came on my property."

"You can't just chain me up."

"Bein' you're chained up, I'd have to disagree."

"What are you gonna do with me?"

"I'm askin' the questions."

He shut the stove door with a clang, stood, and walked toward her. Wakan scooted to the far side of the bed. He pointed a thick finger at her.

"What's an Injun girl doin' sneakin' 'round my cabin?"

"Sneakin'?" She lifted her chin. "I was calling for you."

"So you're supposed to be a distraction?"

He leaned over and peered through a gap in the tattered curtain, scanning the trees outside.

"Are your people after my furs?"

"Furs? No! I'm here alone."

He shook his head and moved back to the stove, pulling down a cast-iron pan and setting it on the burner. He spooned a dollop of lard from a canister and stirred it as it melted.

"Don't give me that. Your reservation's a good ways from here. And what are you? Nine? Ten?"

"I'm twelve. And I made the trip by myself."

He glanced at her, then shook his head again, stirring the pan.

"Fine. So what are you doin' here?"

He tugged at his collar to wipe sweat from his neck. A long, puckered scar circled his throat like a noose mark. Wakan stared at it until he noticed.

When she didn't answer, he turned fully to face her.

"Someone's accusing you of killing...friends of mine," she said.

He held her gaze a moment, then turned back to the stove and shook his head. "Look, kid. People been accusin' me of all sorts of things for a long time now." He faced her again. "Now, if some friends o' yours are dead, well...I'm sorry on that. But I ain't kilt 'em."

He turned back to the pan.

"So if this here little adventure of yours is about gettin' revenge—"

"I know *you* didn't kill them," Wakan cut in. "But I know who did."

He stopped stirring.

"And those very same people are on their way here...right now...to kill you."

The spoon clattered onto the stove top. He turned slowly.

"I think you need to tell me exactly what all this is about," he said. "From the beginning."

Without breaking eye contact, Wakan raised her chained wrist.

He sighed, dug a small key from his shirt pocket, and stepped over to unlock the chain.

Elden

T HE MORNING SUN HUNG low and pale over the blackened ruins of the Josephs' cabin, casting long shadows across the churned, ash-strewn yard. Sheriff Dylan slammed the back door of the undertaker's carriage shut. Inside, two blanket-wrapped bundles lay side by side, dark stains blooming through the rough wool. He rapped twice on the side panel.

The driver—fifties, gaunt, with a face carved from years of hauling the dead—glanced back.

"Take 'em straight to the church," Dylan said. "Chaplain's waitin'."

The driver touched the brim of his hat, slapped the reins, and the horses lurched forward, wheels crunching over frozen ruts as the carriage rolled away.

Dylan stood alone for a moment, staring at the blood-soaked patch of earth where Paul and Audrey had fallen. To his left, a handful of men worked the smoldering remnants of the fire—shovels scraping, boots kicking dirt over glowing embers. The cabin itself was gone: only a heap of charred timbers and twisted nails remained, smoke still curling from the wreckage.

More men moved inside the ruins, digging carefully, searching for anything—or anyone—left behind.

Dylan's gaze settled on one of them: Elden Hinderschott, lean, steady, and clean cut, his face streaked with soot. Their eyes met. Dylan looked away and started walking toward his horse.

Elden dropped his shovel and picked his way out of the rubble, boots crunching over ash.

"Hey, Sheriff!"

Dylan muttered under his breath. "Shit." He kept walking.

"Sheriff!"

Dylan slowed but didn't stop. "Mister Hinderschott. I wanna thank you for comin' out and helpin' with the fire, but if you need to get back to tendin' your store..."

Elden caught up as Dylan reached his horse. "No trouble at all. Eleanor's mindin' the store, and Samantha's old enough to help now."

Dylan nodded once. "Then what can I do for you, Elden?"

"It's just..." Elden glanced at the ruins. "I don't know. Does any of this make any sense at all?"

Dylan regarded him. "I ain't sure a crazy man killin' people's supposed to make sense."

"Okay, but take the fire, for instance. Why'd he set the fire? Cover his tracks? Then why leave the bodies outside? Why not leave 'em where they could burn, too?"

Dylan gave a slight shrug. "Well..."

"And you say he's crazy—that old hermit lives out in the woods. And maybe he is. But he's never hurt anyone up to this point. Why start now? I mean...what does anyone really know about him?"

Dylan turned to face him fully. "What does anyone know about him? Nothin'! 'Cept now we know he's a cold-blooded killer. Our own eyewitness will testify to it."

"Okay, and this witness...Sneed? Really? How reliable a witness is he? He's gotten in more trouble around here than anybody."

Dylan's jaw tightened. "He's kept his nose clean lately."

"And what did he see? Someone ridin' a horse comin' from this general direction?"

"Someone wearin' a bear-skin coat."

"That's what he says. Even so, could he have gotten a good look at the man's face? In the dark?"

"Elden..."

"If I could just talk to Sneed, I could interview him and really discover just what—"

"Enough!"

Dylan jabbed a finger into Elden's chest. Elden took a step back.

"Word is you plan on tryin' your luck as sheriff this next election," Dylan said, voice low and hard. "Maybe you'll win, but I'm bettin' you won't. Either way, for now you leave the sheriffin' to me." He leaned in closer. "My boys are out there right now with orders to bring this Bear-Man fella in alive. An' when they do, I'll find out what's what."

Elden stared back a moment, then nodded. "Sure. Okay."

Dylan looked past him. Prichard was walking up the path from the treeline.

"Now if you'll excuse me," Dylan said, "I've got work to do."

Elden glanced back, saw Prichard, then nodded again. "Sure. Sure."

He turned and walked back toward the ruins, glancing over his shoulder once as Dylan and Prichard met.

When Prichard reached him, the two men leaned close.

"So where are we?" Dylan asked.

"The girl," Prichard said. "She's gone."

Dylan nodded. "Good. And did she lead you to—"

"No. You don't understand."

Their eyes locked.

At the cabin ruins, Elden returned to his spot near Walter, another shoveler helping to gather evidence. They watched Dylan and Prichard talk. Dylan's face darkened; he grabbed Prichard's shirtfront and leaned in, voice rising to a near shout, though the words didn't carry.

Walter whistled low. "Woo! Sheriff looks hoppin' mad. 'Course, I guess we all are, huh?"

Elden kept his eyes on the two men. Dylan jabbed a finger in Prichard's face.

"Killin' the Pastor and his wife the way that guy did," Walter went on.

Dylan stormed off a few steps. Prichard hurried after him.

"No," Walter said. "I wouldn't want to be that Bear Man once Sheriff gets hold of him."

Elden shook his head slowly. "Yeah," he said. "Me neither."

Excuse the Mess

THE BEAR-SKIN COAT LAY in a heap on the dirt floor, still warm from the man's body. Wakan stared at it, then lifted her gaze to the man who had thrown it aside. He moved with quiet purpose, buckling an elaborate gun belt around his waist. He reached for a coiled lasso on the wall—ordinary rope on one end, but the other finished in a heavy, three-pronged steel blade, weighted for throwing. He slid the blade into a custom leather holster on his hip.

"There's a wood box under the bed," he said, voice low. "Get it for me."

He draped two curved metal plates joined by leather straps over his shoulders, buckling the chest and back armor tight.

Wakan didn't move. She watched, transfixed, as the quiet hermit transformed into something harder, sharper.

"Hey!"

She blinked, startled, and crawled beneath the bed. She dragged out a scarred wooden box and set it on the mattress. Inside: two silver six-shooters, barrels etched with tiny skulls, each face frozen in silent agony. Spare cylinders loaded with long, thick bullets rested beside them.

She traced a finger along the skulls. The hermit leaned over, snatched the guns, clicked cylinders into the belt, then held both pistols high. His fingers danced—two sharp *clicks*. He spun the cylinders against his thighs, twirled the revolvers once, and dropped them into the holsters with fluid ease.

Wakan's mouth hung open.

"You're a... trapper?"

He stared at her, silent.

The pots and pans strung along the wall rattled violently.

They both looked toward the noise, then at each other.

"Stay inside," he said.

***

Outside, six riders reined in at the edge of the clearing. Curtis raised a hand; the group dismounted.

"His cabin's just ahead," Curtis said. "We walk it from here."

Rifles came out of scabbards, sidearms checked. The men formed a loose semi-circle around Curtis.

"Plan's simple," he said. "Knock on the door. Get him out in the open. Put him down. Nothin' fancy. Any questions?"

Sneed shifted. "Do we really all need to be here for one man? I could be ten hands deep at Bentley's poker table by now, cash stacked over my head."

Reilly snorted. "Boy, the only thing over your head is how to bluff. You ain't won a poker hand since your daddy was in diapers."

Laughter rippled. Sneed scowled.

Curtis cut it short. "Okay, I know none of us wanna be here. But Sheriff wants a show of force, public-like. Let's get it done quick and be back in town for lunch."

They moved forward.

The cabin sat quiet, smoke curling from the chimney. Skins hung drying, the axe still buried in the bloody stump.

Sneed sniffed the air, then pinched his nose. "We sure he ain't dead already?"

Curtis nodded at the smoke. "Looks like he's here."

He pointed. "Sneed, Giles—each take a side of the porch. Everybody else hang back."

As they moved, Bobby asked, "What are you gonna do?"

"I'm gonna knock on the door."

Curtis took three steps. The door creaked open on its own.

The hermit stepped onto the porch, slow and deliberate. The sun caught the silver of his guns, the glint of the weighted blade at his hip, the hard line of his jaw.

The men froze. This was not the old trapper they expected.

His voice carried calm and low. "I'm sorry. I wasn't expecting company."

He glanced left—Sneed creeping along the porch. Right—Giles doing the same.

He looked back to Curtis. "So I hope you'll excuse the mess."

The next few moments were a blur or violence and death. Among them:

The weighted blade spun free from the hermit's hand, a silver blur trailing a low, mournful whistle through the cold air. It struck Curtis square in the chest with a wet thud, the three prongs sinking deep. Blood sprayed in a bright arc across the porch boards as Curtis staggered, eyes wide, hands clawing uselessly at the rope. The weighted end dragged him backward, jerking him off his feet; the rope snapped taut around the porch post, and his body swung slowly, boots scraping the wood, blood dripping in thick, dark ropes to pool on the frozen ground below.

A frantic figure crashed through the trees, breath ragged, boots pounding over roots and snow. Bullets snapped past, chewing bark into white splinters inches from his face. One round punched through a pine trunk, showering him with hot resin and wood chips. He ducked, stumbled, kept running—until another bullet found his spine. His legs folded; he pitched forward into the snow, face-first, blood blooming beneath him like spilled ink.

Bobby sprinted, arms pumping, eyes wild with terror. "Let's get the hell outta—" The words died as a bullet punched through the back of his skull. The exit wound erupted in a wet explosion of bone fragments and gray-pink brain matter, spraying across the bark of a nearby tree in a glistening fan. Bobby dropped like a cut puppet, limbs twitching once, then still.

Giles crawled on his belly through the ash and dirt, shirt soaked crimson from two ragged holes in his chest. Blood bubbled at his lips with every breath. His fingers scraped toward a dropped rifle. A boot stepped into his line of sight—steady, unhurried. The hermit's shadow fell across him. A single shot rang out. Giles's head jerked sideways, the top of his skull splitting open like a cracked egg, brain spilling in a slow, glistening heap onto the frozen ground.

Eventually...

The woods fell silent once more, broken only by the faint drip of blood on frozen earth.

Town Meeting

THE TOWN SQUARE OF Buffalo Ridge sprawled under a pale noon sky, a rough patchwork of clapboard storefronts, hitching posts, and muddy wheel ruts baked hard by frost. The main street ran dusty and wide, flanked by the livery stable's weathered barn on one end and the steepled church on the other, its whitewash peeling under the harsh Dakota winters. Skinny's Bar—a squat, two-story affair with a sagging balcony and windows yellowed by cigar smoke—sat directly across from the sheriff's office, a sturdier building of grayed timber with a broad porch and a faded sign reading "Sheriff & Jail." The air carried the sharp tang of horse manure, sawdust, and the faint sourness of spilled whiskey.

In front of Skinny's, a crude wooden cowboy loomed near life-size, hat carved at a rakish angle, its face a grotesque attempt at human likeness. Splinters jutted from its edges, and a tin star was nailed to its chest.

Sheriff Dylan's voice cut through the morning chill. "What'd you say this thing is again?"

Skinny, the owner of the establishment, had a grin too wide for his pinched face. He leaned over Dylan's shoulder. "Why, that's you, Sheriff! Ol' Bobby Madale out by the river carved it hisself."

Skinny beamed. Dylan's eyes lingered on the star, then flicked to the carving's uneven smirk.

"I see. And you had a mind to put it out front here?"

"Thought it might help with the next election. Wanted to surprise you with it!"

"Well, 'surprise' ain't exactly the word for what I'm feelin'." Dylan paused, scratching his jaw. "But the election's a bit off yet. Maybe we can move it across the street to my office."

Skinny nodded, pointing to the sheriff's porch. "Yeah! Outside there's a good spot."

"Well, I was thinkin' of puttin' it inside. You know. Keep it out of the weather and all."

Skinny frowned. "Won't many people see it inside."

Dylan gave the carving a final glance—its empty eyes seemed to mock him. He slapped Skinny's arm. "You know. 'Til the election."

He turned and froze. A crowd had gathered in the street—two dozen townsfolk, faces drawn and grim, their coats dusted with trail dirt. More were coming, boots scuffing the boardwalks, voices murmuring low. Dylan caught Prichard's eye across the square. Prichard gave a curt nod.

"Ladies and gentlemen," Dylan called, stepping to the edge of Skinny's porch, "I appreciate you comin' out. All of you know what this is about, so I won't go into all the details. Our own

Man-of-the-Lord...our good friend...Reverend Josephs and his lovely wife, Audrey, were gunned down late last night in cold blood."

The crowd stirred—heads shook, lips tightened, a few women dabbed eyes with handkerchiefs. The news wasn't new, but the weight of it still landed heavy. Among them stood Elden Hinderschott, his wife Eleanor at his side, their daughter Samantha—fourteen, pale and wide-eyed—clutching her mother's sleeve. Dylan's gaze lingered on Elden, then moved on.

"Now, I don't know the whys and the what-fors, but I do know who killed 'em. I got a witness to that."

Gasps rippled through the crowd. Faces turned to neighbors, whispers rising. Not everyone had heard this part.

"And I got my men out there, right now, hunting the killer down!"

Clapping broke out, sharp and eager.

"Yeah!" a man shouted from the back.

"String 'im up by his balls!" another bellowed.

The crowd erupted—hoots, hollers, more clapping. Dylan stood taller, chest puffed, nodding as if leading a congregation.

Elden's voice cut through. "What's gonna happen to him, Sheriff?"

Dylan's eyes found him. Elden stood calm, arms crossed.

"When your men bring him in," Elden pressed. "What happens then?"

Dylan sucked his teeth, irritation flaring.

"What happens then is we hang 'im in front of the church and let the vultures have at 'im!" the second man yelled.

The crowd roared approval. Elden dropped his gaze, jaw tight. Dylan's mouth twitched into a crooked smile. He raised his hands for quiet.

"Now, now, let's quiet down. Mr. Hinderschott here brings up a good and valid point. We are a law-abidin' community, and, witness or no, the killer will get a fair and honest trial."

Groans rolled through the crowd like a low thunder.

"Yes. Yes, he will. So long as he gives himself up and comes in quietly..."

Dylan's voice trailed off. In the distance, beyond the crowd, three riders rounded the corner of the livery. Reilly and Sneed rode upright, faces grim. Willie slumped in his saddle, one arm hanging limp, blood staining his shirt. A third horse trailed behind, riderless.

Whispers spread as heads turned.

Dylan leaned toward Prichard. "Tell them to head to my cabin."

"Looks like Willie's hurt," Prichard said. "The doctor—"

Through gritted teeth: "My cabin. Now!"

Prichard nodded and slipped off the porch, weaving through the crowd toward the riders.

"Folks! Folks, I've got business to attend to, if you please." Dylan turned to Skinny. "Skinny, let's get everyone a drink."

He faced the crowd again, forcing a smile. "On me."

Clapping broke out again, softer this time. The townsfolk began filing into Skinny's, boots thumping on the boardwalk. Dylan shook a few outstretched hands, nodding, his eyes flicking to Prichard leading the riders down a side street, away from the square.

He kept smiling, but his grip tightened on the last hand he shook.

The Devil of Black Hills

I N THE BACK ROOM of Sheriff Dylan's cabin, a single lantern hung from a nail in the rafter, throwing weak yellow light over the scene. Reilly sat on the dirt floor, cradling Willie in his lap. Willie's shirt was soaked dark, his breathing shallow and wet. Sneed paced near the wall, chewing his thumbnail raw. Prichard sat at the scarred table, a tin cup of whiskey untouched in front of him, eyes distant.

Dylan burst through the door, coat still on. "Okay, somebody tell me what the hell's goin' on. Where's everybody?"

Prichard didn't look up. "Dead."

Dylan stopped short. "What! There were six of you goin' after one man. What happened?"

Sneed's voice cracked. "We were ambushed."

"Ambushed? He had people with 'im?"

The hermit's back, coat flaring as he drew both silver guns in a single blur of motion, barrels catching the sun.

Sneed swallowed hard. "Yes...No...I don't know. I only saw him. Him and...and..."

Willie's voice rasped, barely audible. "The girl."

Reilly pressed a hand to Willie's chest. "Stay still. Don't try to talk."

Dylan's eyes narrowed. "What girl?"

Reilly glanced up. "Willie claims he saw a girl there. Injun girl. But in his condition, with you tellin' us about the girl in the shed...he could be imaginin'—"

Willie tried to sit up, eyes glassy. "I saw her! She was there!"

"Shhhh," Reilly soothed. "Settle down now."

Dylan looked around the room, mind turning. "Well, that explains it, don't it? Willie did see a girl. The girl from last night. She went out and warned him you were comin', which is why he got the jump on you."

Reilly's voice was tight. "Sheriff, we gotta get Willie to the doctor quick."

Dylan waved him off. "In a minute." He paced. "Now if that girl's with him, then he knows everything. So we can't just let this go."

Prichard finally spoke. "Weren't plannin' on it."

"Of course not."

Dylan clapped his hands once. "What do we know about him?"

He looked at Reilly, who nodded toward Sneed.

Sneed's voice was small. "He's fast. I ain't never seen nobody that fast."

The hermit's guns roaring in rapid succession, smoke curling from the barrels.

Dylan reached the stove, grabbed the coffee pot. "Okay. What else?"

Sneed swallowed. "And he's got these strange guns."

On the barrel, tiny skulls etched along the metal seeming to scream in the muzzle flash.

Reilly shook his head. "I ain't got a look at his guns."

Sneed's eyes were wide. "I did. Hell, they was pointed right at me."

The barrel swung toward him, skulls glinting.

Dylan poured coffee, sloshing it over the rim. "I don't care about his guns. Every body who thinks he's a gunslinger's got fancy guns. What else?"

Reilly looked at Sneed. "You see his neck?"

Sneed shook his head.

Reilly turned to Dylan. "He had this scar around his neck. Almost like a rope burn."

The hermit on the porch, coat open, the thick, puckered scar circling his throat like a noose's ghost.

Dylan set the pot down hard. It clattered. He turned.

Reilly shrugged. "It was almost like...like somebody tried to hang him, but...I dunno."

Dylan and Prichard exchanged a look. Prichard sat up straighter.

Prichard's voice was low as he looked toward Sneed. "Tell us more about his guns."

Sneed shifted. "Sheriff says he don't wanna hear about the guns."

Dylan snapped, "Just tell us about the damn guns!"

Sneed shuffled. "Well...now, ever'thing happened real fast, but...they was silver. And they had round things on the barrel. Like...like..."

Prichard leaned forward. "Skulls?"

Sneed nodded. "Yeah. Maybe."

Dylan and Prichard locked eyes. Dylan moved to a cabinet, yanked open a drawer, and started rifling through papers. "What else? What else about him?"

Reilly's voice rose. "Sheriff, Willie's lookin' real bad—"

"Not now, Reilly! Sneed, what else?"

Dylan slapped a stack of papers on the counter. Sneed kept talking.

"Well...there was this lasso. He kept swingin' it around. Had something heavy and sharp on the end of it."

The hermit advancing, the weighted blade spinning lazily on the rope, catching the light.

Prichard stood. "It's him. Dammit, it's him!"

Dylan found what he was looking for—a worn wanted poster—and held it up. Prichard leaned in. They stared at each other, then Dylan turned the poster for the others.

"This him?"

Reilly studied it a moment. "Maybe."

He looked to Sneed. Sneed nodded. "Yeah. I think so. He's got more hair now, but I think that's him."

Dylan read the poster himself, jaw tightening. "Jesus..."

Silence settled, thick as smoke.

Sneed broke it. "Well? Who is he?"

Dylan exhaled hard. "No one knows who he is. No name I ever heard, anyway. He was a wanted man some fifteen or so years ago. Had a high bounty on his head. Everybody was gunnin' for him. Hell, me and Prichard, too."

Reilly's eyes widened. "Wanted? Where?"

Prichard's voice was flat. "Everywhere. For any number of crimes. Robbery, theft...murder."

Sneed's voice trembled. "And no one knows who he is?"

Dylan shook his head. "Well, he's been called many things, de-pendin' on where you live. South of the border, they call him La Mano del Diablo. Folks in parts of Texas call him The Angel of Death. Little east o' here, he's known as the Arkansas Demon. But round these parts, he's the Devil of Black Hills."

The room went still. Only Willie's ragged breathing broke the quiet.

Dylan forced a chuckle. "Well...from the change of mood, I'm guessing you all's heard of him."

Reilly spoke softly. "I'll tell you what I heard. Down in Santa Fe...twenty men stood around him, guns drawn. Had 'im dead to rights. Twenty men. To his twelve bullets." He paused. "In the end, the sand was wet and red with their blood, and the Devil walked away without so much as a scratch."

Dylan's laugh was weaker. "Stories. You can't go believin' ever'thing you—"

Sneed cut in. "My daddy used to tell me about 'im."

All eyes turned to him.

"When we was livin' over in Sheridan, Wyoming. Daddy told me that he ain't no man at all. That he cain't be killed. That he's an evil spirit that was spat out of the bowls of hell."

Reilly corrected quietly. "Bowels."

Sneed ignored him. "They say that if you look in his eyes and survive, that he'll hunt you down for all eternity, 'cause ain't nobody supposed to see his face."

The hermit turning his head, eyes locking on Sneed—cold, unblinking, burning into him.

Sneed's breath hitched. "Christ, Sheriff! I looked right in his eyes!"

Dylan waved a hand. "Settle down, okay. Ain't no reason to get yourself all worked up over—"

Willie gasped, voice weak. "I'll tell you what I heard."

Reilly pressed his hand harder. "Willie, don't. You gotta save your strength."

Willie's eyes fluttered. "They say his guns were taken in a gunfight...with Satan hisself. They say can't no one fire them but him, because only a man with as cold...and heartless a soul as his can pull them triggers."

He gasped again.

Reilly looked up. "Sheriff."

Dylan shook his head. Willie kept going.

"An' I heard...an' I believe this...any man killed by a bullet from one o' his guns...their soul will forever burn in the lowest...hottest...depths of hell."

Silence again. Only Willie's labored breathing.

Dylan's voice was sharp. "This is good news. Don't you guys see that? Ain't nobody gonna doubt that he killed the reverend and his wife now. We'll be able to pull together a full-on posse! Everyone will want to be a part of taking down the Devil of Black Hills!"

He snatched the poster, jabbed a finger at the $5000 bounty. "An' you see this? This ain't nothing but pocket change. Our clients will pay top dollar to be a part of this hunt. Ever' one of 'em, top dollar! All that on top of the bounty!"

No one spoke.

Dylan turned to Reilly. "You understand me, don't cha, Reilly?"

Reilly nodded uncertainly.

"Sneed?"

Sneed stared at the floor, chewing his nail. "I saw his face."

The hermit's eyes, locked on him—unblinking, endless.

Dylan's voice sharpened. "Sneed?"

Sneed looked up. "Sheriff. I...I need to go home."

Dylan stared. "Well...you're probably tired, I get that, but right now I need—"

"No. Home. To Wyoming."

Dylan's laugh was brittle. "Look. I know you're a bit shook up. We all are. But we can't just turn tail and...and—"

Sneed stepped forward. "I saw his face, Sheriff! I saw it! Now, does that mean I believe all that stuff about him, this Devil-man? I don't know. But can I take that kinda chance? What if we go after him and he shoots me! What if what Willie says is true! I don't wanna burn in hell for all eternity!"

Dylan shook his head. "So...what? You wanna head West to home? Run back to Daddy? You forget that he kicked you out all those years ago? Left you to fend for yourself? You forget who took you in? Who treated you like a son when you had nothin'!?!"

Sneed stared at the floor, then shook his head. "No. No, sir. I ain't forgot. But, Daddy, he turned me out when I was a lawbreaker—"

"You're a lawbreaker now."

"Yeah. Yeah, I am, Sheriff. But I ain't got to be no more. My momma and daddy, they're good, church-goin' people. An' I could go home an'...an' git right with God."

Dylan stared at him a long moment. He looked at Prichard, who sat back down and picked up his drink. Then Dylan turned back.

"You know...the only thing more dangerous than a lawbreaker...is a righteous one."

Sneed stared, not catching it. Then it hit him. "No. No, Sheriff. You ain't got nothin' to worry about there. I would never talk to anyone about the things we done."

Dylan said nothing. Sneed looked to Prichard. "Prichard. Reilly. Ya'll got my word, now. Ya'll know me. Ya'll know I ain't no two-bit squealer."

Dylan turned back to the stove, poured coffee again. "Understand something. If you leave, you stay gone. You don't come back."

Sneed deflated. "Sheriff. There ain't no need…"

Dylan spun and hurled the coffee pot at the wall near Sneed's head. It toppled to the floor, dented, hot coffee splashing everywhere. Sneed stumbled back, nearly tripping over a chair.

Dylan closed the distance fast, grabbing Sneed by the collar. "You hear me, you yellow-bellied son-of-a-bitch! You ride out a' here, and you ride fast! And if I ever see your face within a hundred miles of Buffalo Ridge, I'll put a bullet in it!"

He shoved Sneed toward the door. "Now, git out of my sight!"

Sneed fumbled for the knob, hands shaking. "Thank you, Sheriff. I'm sorry."

The door shut behind him. Dylan kicked it hard, then snatched the pot from the floor.

"Anybody else feel like runnin'? Huh? Anybody else had the fear of God put in them 'cause of *one man!*? Reilly?"

Reilly shook his head.

"Prichard?"

Prichard set his drink down hard. "Who do you think you're talking to?" He leaned forward. "I've heard all these stories about the Devil of Black Hills, and a hundred more just like 'em. But what's true and what ain't don't make no difference to me."

He met Dylan's eyes. "That bastard killed three of my men. So I plan on killing him with his own gun…and sending his ass back to hell."

Dylan nodded.

Reilly's voice was quiet. "Four of your men."

They looked. Willie's eyes stared blankly at the ceiling. Reilly gently closed his eyelids.

Dylan stared a moment, anger rising. He strode to the window, grabbed a rifle leaning against the wall, and threw open the shutters.

In the distance, Sneed galloped away, dust trailing behind him.

Dylan lifted the rifle and fired. Sneed pitched from the saddle, body tumbling into the dirt.

Dylan tossed the rifle onto the table. "Make it five."

He grabbed the wanted poster. "Reilly, get to the printers and have 'im make a hundred more of these. Then send out men in every direction. I want these hung in every town within forty miles by morning."

Reilly stood, blood-soaked clothes dark against his skin.

Dylan glanced at him. "It's fine. Let 'em see you like that. It'll motivate 'em."

Reilly took the poster. Prichard stood.

Dylan's voice was hard. "Prichard, you and me are gonna hit every one of our clients, one by one. Let 'em know there's a new hunt on."

He looked around the room, a grim smile splitting his face. "Biggest one yet."

On the Run

THE LATE AFTERNOON SUN slanted low through the pines, painting the clearing around the hermit's cabin in long, bloody streaks of savageness. Bodies lay scattered across the frozen ground like broken dolls—Curtis swinging gently from the porch rail, blood frozen in dark rivulets down his shirt; Bobby sprawled face-down in the snow, skull split open; Giles crumpled near the woodpile, brains leaking from the top of his head like spilled porridge. The air stank of gunpowder, copper, and the sour tang of voided bowels.

Wakan stood at the bottom of the porch steps, small frame rigid, mouth open, eyes wide as she took in the carnage. Her breath fogged in sharp, shallow bursts.

The cabin door creaked. The Devil stepped out, a full rucksack slung over one shoulder, rifle cradled in the crook of his arm. He didn't glance at her, didn't pause—just walked past, boots crunching over blood-crusted snow, heading straight for the treeline.

Wakan blinked, then hurried after him, half-running to keep up.

"Why'd you send their horses away?" she asked, voice small but steady. "Don't we need them?"

"First," he said without turning, "ain't no 'we.' Second, can't cover horse tracks. Best to head out on foot. They'll spend a day followin' the horses before they realize there's no one on 'em."

Wakan glanced back at the clearing, then at the dense wall of trees ahead. "What's the best direction to head?"

He stopped, scanned the woods with a slow sweep of his head. "Well. Your settlement's north o' here. They'll be coverin' that way, hopin' to catch you headed home. Town's south. You definitely don't wanna go into town. I'd head west."

He started walking again, long strides eating distance. Wakan hesitated, looking north, then south, then west, confusion creasing her brow. She jogged to catch up.

"Why not east?"

"'Cause I'm headed east," he said over his shoulder, "and I'd prefer you go in the opposite direction that I am."

She stopped dead, boots sinking into the snow. He kept going.

"Hey!" she called. "Wait!"

He didn't slow. "Don't wait too long before you leave. It'll be dark soon, and you don't want to be wanderin' these woods alone at night."

"But...I saved your life!"

He stopped then, turned fully. She halted a few paces away, chest heaving. "Why?" he asked. "'Cause you warned me they was comin'? Kid, you didn't save me, you killed them. I ain't never been one to need savin'."

Wakan looked back toward the bodies. Her shoulders slumped.

He watched her a moment, then jerked his chin toward the hanging carcasses near the cabin—deer, elk, a few smaller game, flies already buzzing thick around them.

"Look, kid. You found your way here, you can find your way home. You're just gonna have to...find a different way." He pointed. "Feel free to take somethin' with you to eat for the trip. Just gonna go bad otherwise."

Wakan glanced at a gutted deer hanging from a tree, its eyes glazed, flies crawling over the raw meat. When she looked up again, the hermit was gone—engulfed by the trees as though he'd never been there.

***

Night had fallen over the town of Buffalo Ridge, the main street lit only by the glow of lanterns in windows and the occasional flare of a match. Elden Hinderschott turned the key in the lock of his general store, the brass bell above the door jingling faintly. He reached to flip the "Open" sign to "Closed."

Through the glass, he saw movement across the street—Reilly standing on the boardwalk in front of the sheriff's office, handing out fliers to a growing knot of men. Lantern light caught the blood still staining Reilly's shirt, dark and unmistakable. Horses stamped, saddles creaked as riders mounted and spurred away at a gallop.

Elden paused, then unlocked the door again and stepped outside.

Reilly's voice carried across the square. "Take one. Take several. Post 'em anywhere and everywhere. Let folks know the sheriff's holdin' a town meeting first thing tomorrow morning."

Elden approached. Reilly handed him a wanted poster without looking up, already turning to the next man.

Elden stepped aside, unfolded the sheet. A horrifying figure stared up at him—a scarred-neck and face; hard, dead eyes. The wanted poster was one he recognized. But he hasn't seen it in a long time. The bold text below the photo read:

WANTED: DEVIL OF BLACK HILLS
$5000 REWARD DEAD OR ALIVE

Elden stared at the poster a long moment, then looked up. Reilly was still handing out sheets, voice rising over the murmurs of the crowd. Riders peeled off into the night, posters clutched in gloved hands, heading north, south, east, west—spreading the name like a fever.

Elden folded the poster carefully and slipped it into his coat pocket. He turned back toward his store, the bell jingling softly as he stepped inside and locked the door behind him.

Two Gods

T HE FIRE CRACKLED LOW in the small clearing, its glow barely holding back the pressing dark of the dense forest. The Devil sat cross-legged on a fallen log, close enough to feel the heat on his scarred neck. A skinned rabbit roasted over the flames on a makeshift spit of green willow, fat dripping and hissing as it hit the coals. He reached over with his knife, sliced off a steaming chunk of meat, and chewed it slowly, eyes fixed on the shadows beyond the light.

A twig snapped.

He sighed. "I told you not to follow me."

Wakan stepped from the bushes into the firelight, small and shivering, her breath fogging in the cold. She looked from him to the rabbit, eyes wide with hunger.

"I don't know the way home."

He studied her a moment, then jerked his chin toward a flat rock near the fire. "Come on. Pull up a rock."

She approached cautiously, sat on the edge of the stone, hands clasped tight in her lap. Her gaze stayed locked on the meat.

The Devil cut off a larger piece, stabbed it with the knife, and held it out to her. Wakan stared at it, then snatched it with both hands and tore into it, eating fast and messy.

"Slow down," he said. "It's dead. It ain't goin' nowhere."

She tried to slow, but her hunger won out.

"So you made the trip all the way here," he said, cutting himself another bite, "but you don't know how to get back?" He chewed, watching her. "You said your daddy sent you to trade for a horse?"

Wakan stopped eating, eyes dropping to the ground. "I wasn't being completely honest with you when I told you that."

"You don't say." He took another bite. "Does your daddy even know you came?"

She swallowed hard. "My father's been missing for a month."

He stopped chewing.

"He left the village alone to make the trade for the horse on my behalf," she continued, voice small. "But he never came back. And since Pastor Josephs didn't mention him, he never arrived either. I came to find him."

The Devil resumed chewing, slower now. "And your momma was okay with that?"

"She didn't know I was leaving."

He thought about that, then kept eating. "Well, might shoulda told her your plans. She woulda saved you the trouble. If your daddy ain't come home in a month, then he's dead."

Wakan closed her eyes. Her shoulders shook. A soft sob escaped her.

The Devil sighed, shook his head. "Sorry. I didn't mean to..."

He watched her cry for a moment, then spoke again, quieter. "My own daddy died when I was about your age. Kilt dead for dealin' from the bottom of a deck."

Wakan looked up, wiping her eyes. "Were you sad?"

"Sad that I weren't gettin' whooped every day? Not really."

She lowered her head again, nibbling at the meat while tears fell. The Devil watched her quietly.

"Look," he said finally. "You can sleep here tonight. Keep warm by the fire. In the mornin', I'll point you the right direction. That sound okay?"

Wakan nodded slowly. He stood, stretched, patted his belly, and dug through his pack. He pulled out a rolled blanket and spread it near the fire.

Wakan watched him. "My name's Wakan. Well, my real name's Wakanyeja Wicayazanpi, but most people just call me Wakan."

He snorted. "I can see why."

"Do you have a name?"

He paused, fiddling with the blanket. "Eat all you want. It's just gonna go bad."

***

The fire was beginning to flair again as the Devil had just added new wood to it. Wakan lay on the blanket, curled on her side, staring into it. The Devil leaned against a tree, belt and weapons on the ground beside him, using a stick to pick his teeth.

She turned onto her back. "You're not worried about the fire?"

He glanced at the flames, then at her.

"That someone might see it," she added.

He looked up through the canopy, where the trees closed tight overhead. "Nah. Now, if it was daylight, folks could see the smoke for miles away. But at night...with all the trees above us...light gets blocked."

Wakan nodded, then stared up at the stars visible through the branches. "My father once told me that there are many, many gods. Maybe as many as all the stars in the sky. But I don't know if that sounds right."

The Devil kept cleaning his teeth.

"Then Reverend Josephs, he said there was only one God. A jealous and angry God who should be feared. But that doesn't sound right either." She looked at him. "Which do you think is right?"

He thought for a moment, still working the stick. "There's two gods I know of. One for each hip."

He paused. "An' they got twelve disciples between 'em."

Another pause. "And when those disciples go to preachin'...well...fear's just the beginnin'."

Wakan stared back up at the stars. After a while she asked, "Where you gonna sleep?"

He tossed the stick aside. "Well, Little Missy, that's one thing you'll learn about me real quick: if somebody's gunnin' for me...I don't sleep."

***

Morning light filtered pale through the trees. The Devil leaned against the same tree, head tipped back, snoring loudly, mouth open, a thin trail of drool glistening on his beard.

Wakan stood over him, staring down. Her eyes drifted to his gun belt and weapons on the ground. She crouched, ran a hand along the barrel of one pistol, tracing the tiny skulls etched into the metal. Then she lifted the weighted blade on the end of his lasso, dried blood still caked along the prongs.

Her gaze fell on a wooden handle sticking out of his rucksack. She eased it open and lifted out a small hatchet.

***

A thick tree trunk. The hatchet struck it with a dull *thump* and fell to the ground.

Wakan walked over, picked it up, paced back twenty steps, aimed, and threw again. It clattered harmlessly to the roots.

As she bent to retrieve it:

"Hatchet's good for choppin' things," the Devil's voice said behind her.

She turned. He was buckling his gun belt, eyes on her.

"But I wouldn't wanna have to throw one to save my life."

She walked back to her spot. "My father can stick it about seven out of ten times."

She threw again. Same result. The Devil nodded.

"Even so, it's those three outta ten that'll get ya killed."

He walked over, pulling one of his pistols. "Now looky here." He held it out flat on his palm. "You use this to throw a bullet, an' it'll stick. Every time."

Wakan studied the gun, hands behind her back.

"Wanna see somethin' really neat? Reach out there and pull the trigger."

She hesitated, then shook her head.

"Go on, now. It won't bite."

She reached slowly, fingers hovering, then pulled back, shaking her head again.

"Okay, look." He popped the cylinder open, emptied the bullets into his other hand, showed her the empty chambers. "It's empty. S ee?"

Wakan peered down the cylinder and nodded.

He clicked it back into place and held the gun out again. "Now, then. Pull the trigger."

She reached out, touched the trigger with one finger, and pulled. Nothing.

"Go on, put some muscle behind it."

She used both hands, straining. The trigger didn't budge.

"Let me show you somethin'." He leaned down, held the grip so she could see. On the back, he pressed a metal strip. Four small buttons popped out from the front.

Wakan's eyes widened.

"Now, watch. Top two." He pressed the top two. "Bottom two." He pressed those. "Top and bottom." He pressed those. "Bottom three." He pressed the bottom three. A soft *click* sounded.

Wakan's mouth opened.

"Now pull the trigger."

She reached out, dry-fired it with one finger. The hammer fell with a sharp snap.

"What is that?"

"It's a sorta combination lockin' mechanism. Had these guns made special by a gunsmith down in Laredo who owed me a favor."

"What'd he owe you a favor for?"

He looked at her, a flicker of irritation. "Never mind that. Can you remember the combination?"

Wakan thought. "Top two...bottom two..."

"Yeah..."

"Top and bottom...bottom three."

"That's it. Now, don't you go tellin' that to anybody. It's a secret for just us, okay?"

She smiled and nodded. He started reloading the pistol. She frowned.

"Are you going to point me the way home now?"

He kept loading. "Suppose I should."

Her shoulders sagged. He noticed.

"But why don't we eat somethin' first. Watcha say?"

Wakan brightened, nodded. The Devil stood sharply, suddenly aware, and listened.

Wakan frowned. "What?"

He walked away, still loading his gun.

The Rousey Family

THE DEVIL AND WAKAN lay flat on their stomachs along the rocky edge of an outcrop, the dense forest dropping away sharply below them into a wide, sun-dappled valley. Through a spyglass, the scene sharpened into focus: three riders moving at a steady trot across a distant clearing, their horses kicking up faint puffs of dust from the frozen earth. Leading them was Len Rousey, his face etched with the deep lines of a life spent chasing bounties under harsh skies. Flanking him were two of his sons, Kurt and Hank, both broad-shouldered and silent, rifles resting easy across their saddles like extensions of their arms.

Wakan's whisper broke the quiet. "Who is it?"

The Devil kept the glass pressed to his eye. "Rouseys. Family of bounty hunters."

"Bounty hunters?"

He passed the spyglass to her. She adjusted it clumsily at first, then peered through, her breath catching at the magnified figures.

"Think they're looking for us?" she asked.

He nodded, "Have to assume so. But the Rouseys ain't from Buffalo Ridge. They're out along Deadwood ways. Which means news is travelin' fast."

Wakan set the glass down, her dark eyes meeting his. "Well, they're way down there. We can easily miss them if we circle around."

The Devil didn't answer immediately, his gaze fixed on the riders below, something unspoken tightening his jaw.

"What's wrong?" she pressed.

"Rousey family's a group of five. Four boys and their daddy. So where's the other two?"

Before he could say more, the cold steel of a rifle barrel pressed hard into the nape of his neck.

Flem Rousey's voice rang out, sharp and triumphant. "Daddy sent us to scout ahead."

The Devil closed his eyes for a brief second, cursing inwardly. Wakan's face went pale, her wide eyes darting between him and the unseen threat.

"Now, turn around," Flem ordered. "Slow-like."

They rolled onto their backs with deliberate care, hands raised in surrender. Standing over them was Flem Rousey, a skinny young man, clean-shaven and buzzing with eager energy, his rifle trained steady on the Devil's chest. Beside him hulked Len Jr., a mountain of a man with a full, tangled beard, his expression blank except for the occasional low grunt that rumbled from his throat like distant th under.

Flem's grin split his face wide. "It's him, Len! I told you!"

Len Jr. grunted in response, stepping forward to kick the Devil's weapons into a haphazard pile—the silver revolvers, the coiled lasso, the hatchet Wakan had been practicing with.

Flem kept babbling, his words tumbling out in excitement. "We live up yonder mountain, and when I saw the light of your fire last night..."

Wakan shot a glance at the Devil, who could only offer a faint shrug.

"I told my daddy, 'Daddy, that there's the Devil! I just know it.'"

Wakan's brow furrowed at the name, confusion flickering across her features.

"'Course, Len here thought I was crazy," Flem went on. "Says could be anybody out in those woods. But I knew it was the Devil."

Flem caught Wakan's puzzled look and laughed. "What? You don't know who this is? This here's the Devil of Black Hills! The meanest, deadliest outlaw this side of... of... hell, anything!"

Wakan turned her gaze to the Devil, searching his face, but he avoided her eyes, staring instead at the rifle barrel.

"Folks been lookin' for him for more'n fifteen years now!" Flem crowed. "Wanted for killin' people all over. Men, women, children. You name it, he done kilt it!"

Len Jr. finished gathering the weapons, tossing them farther out of reach. Flem's attention snagged on the silver revolvers.

"Hey! Is that those guns I'm always hearin' about?"

He edged closer, rifle still leveled, and bent to scoop one up, whistling low as he turned it in the light.

Len Jr.'s voice was a growl. "Watch 'em, now!"

"I got 'em, I got 'em," Flem replied, though his eyes lingered on the pistol. He whistled a high pitch, "I don't care what Daddy says. I'm keepin' these.

"You'll do what you're told, dammit!" Len Jr. barked. Then he turned back to the embankment.

Flem winked at the Devil. "He's probably right. These here pistols likely to go for a good—hey, would you look at that!"

He kept the rifle on them with one hand while grabbing the weighted end of the lasso with the other. He started to spin it experimentally over his head, the blade whistling faintly as it picked up speed.

"Wow! Still got blood on it and everything!"

He glanced over at Len Jr., who had moved to the embankment's edge, waving his arms to signal the riders far below in the valley.

"Hey, what you think we should do with the Injun girl?" Flem called.

Len Jr. kept signaling, jumping slightly to catch attention. "Sheriff in Buffalo Ridge wants her."

"Yeah, I know," Flem said, the lasso spinning faster now, a blur of rope and steel. "But he don't have to know we found her. Ain't no bounty on her head, far's I know."

Len Jr. looked back long enough to grunt again, "You'll do what you're told."

"Yeah. Okay. But hear me out. I got this guy down in Loosiana might wanna buy her."

Wakan's breath hitched, her eyes darting from Flem to the Devil, who remained still as stone, muscles coiled.

"Now, he mostly trades in niggers," Flem continued, the lasso whirling even quicker, "but he's always said if I run across any Injuns, 'specially purty ones—"

Len Jr. whistled sharply down the valley. "Think they saw me."

Flem's eyes flicked toward his brother for a split second. It was all the Devil needed. His boot lashed out, connecting with Flem's knee in a sickening crunch. Flem yelped, the lasso flying wild. The weighted blade whipped around his own body in a frenzy, the prongs burying deep into the side of his head with a wet thud. Blood sprayed as he crumpled, rifle discharging harmlessly into the branches above.

Len Jr. spun at the sound. "What the hell, Flem..."

Wakan and the Devil dove for the weapons pile. Wakan reached the hatchet first, her fingers closing around the handle. She hurled it with all her might at Len Jr.

The blade smacked flat against his massive chest and clattered to the ground.

The Devil's voice was dry amid the chaos. "What'd I tell you?"

Len Jr. snarled, yanking his sidearm free. The Devil's hand closed on a revolver. Two shots rang out in quick succession—center mass. Len Jr. staggered, blood blooming across his shirt, then toppled backward over the embankment, body tumbling down the slope in a cascade of dirt and leaves.

The Devil rose, buckling his gun belt as he scanned the valley. "Their horses must be around here someplace. Look over there."

Wakan nodded and darted into the brush. He watched her disappear, a thoughtful expression crossing his face, then turned to yank the lasso free from Flem's corpse, the body flopping limply as the rope unwound.

He spotted Flem's rifle lying nearby and picked it up, checking the chamber with practiced efficiency.

Down on the wagon trail below, Len Sr., Kurt, and Hank galloped hard, guns already drawn, dust swirling in their wake. The sharp crack of gunshots echoed from above, halting them in their t racks.

Len Sr.'s voice was grim. "That's Flem's rifle. Come on!"

They spurred their horses faster, leaning low over the saddles.

Back at the overlook, the Devil fired three more deliberate shots into the air, the reports cracking like thunder through the trees.

Wakan emerged from the brush leading a stolen horse by the reins. "What are you doing?"

He lowered the rifle. "You know how to ride a horse? I mean, really ride."

She nodded with quiet confidence, swinging up into the saddle.

He climbed on behind her. "You take the reins. Head that way."

He pointed down the slope, toward the trail.

"But...won't they be coming from that way?"

The Devil nodded. "Ain't no use runnin' now. We're gonna have to go through 'em."

Wakan slapped the reins, and the horse surged forward.

On the trail, Len Sr., Kurt, and Hank rounded a bend, eyes scanning the trees. Suddenly, Wakan and the Devil exploded from the brush to their right, the horse leaping over a fallen log in a spray

of snow and leaves. The Devil swung the lasso over his head in a w
ide arc.

Time seemed to stretch as the rope sailed out, looping cleanly
around Hank's neck. In the same fluid motion, the Devil hurled
the weighted end upward, where it caught a thick overhead limb
and wrapped tight.

He leaped from the saddle, snagging the falling end of the rope.
His weight yanked it taut. Hank was jerked skyward, feet kicking
wildly, neck straining against the noose as his horse bolted away
riderless.

Still airborne, the Devil drew a pistol and fired twice. Kurt took
the first shot to the chest, staggering in the saddle; the second
punched through his forehead, body pitching backward in a life-
less arc, blood misting the air.

Len Sr. took aim, but his horse reared in panic, and his shot
went wide into the trees. The animal bucked again, throwing him
hard to the ground. It came down on his chest with a crunch of
bone, then scrambled up and trampled him in its terror—hooves
pounding ribs and limbs—before galloping off into the woods.

The Devil landed lightly, boots hitting the trail with a puff of
dust. Len Sr. lay in the dirt, mangled and gasping, blood frothing
at his mouth.

"You son of a..."

He clawed weakly for his pistol, his spine broken. "You kilt my
boys!"

The Devil stepped over him, pistol leveled at his head.

"You bastard! You kilt my—"

The shot echoed, silencing him forever.

The Devil stared down at the body for a long moment, breath steady. Then two bullets kicked up dirt near his feet.

He whirled. Hank—still hanging from the limb, face swollen and purple—had somehow drawn his revolver and fired blindly. The Devil returned fire twice, the shots slamming into Hank's chest. His body went limp, swaying gently.

The Devil yanked the weighted blade free from the tree, Hank's corpse dropping in a heavy thud. He coiled the rope methodically, buckling it back onto his belt.

Wakan stood nearby, holding their horse's reins, her eyes fixed on him with a mix of awe and uncertainty.

As he straightened: "Is it true what that man said about you? That you're an outlaw with a bounty on your head?"

The Devil met her gaze. "It is."

"Was he right about what you've done? That you've killed women and children?"

He took a slow breath, then started toward her. She took a step back. He stopped, hands out in a gesture of peace.

"Hey. I ain't gonna hurt you. Now I promised you I'd point you the way home. I can still do that, and if you ride hard, you might can be there in a day. Maybe day and a half. But I can't promise you'll make it at all. They'll be lots of people lookin' for me."

A beat.

"Lookin' for us," he added.

Wakan lowered her head, fingers tight on the reins.

"But if you'll let me, I know someone who I think can help us. Give us a place to lay low until things cool down."

Another beat.

"It'll mean back-trackin' a bit, but I think it's your best bet."

Wakan stared at him, weighing his words.

"We can trust 'em?"

The distant rattle of a wagon echoed up the trail—two men on the driver's seat, another peering from the canvas back.

The Devil glanced at it. "We gotta move."

They ran for the trees as the wagon ground to a halt.

The driver's head whipped toward the bodies scattered on the trail.

"Holy shit!"

Posse

THE INTERIOR OF SKINNY'S Bar was thick with the smell of stale whiskey, wet wool coats, and the sharp tang of unwashed men who had ridden hard for days. Lanterns hung from blackened rafters, casting a smoky amber glow over the crowded room. Rough tables were pushed back against the walls to make space, and every stool, bench, and standing spot was filled with bounty hunters—lean, scarred men with hard eyes and harder hands, their coats crusted with trail dust, sidearms worn low and easy. More kept pushing through the batwing doors, boots thudding on the worn pine floor, each new arrival scanning the room like a wolf sniffing for blood.

Sheriff Dylan leaned against the bar, arms crossed, watching the growing throng with a practiced calm. Prichard stood a few paces away, his back to the wall, arms folded, eyes flicking over the faces of the newcomers. At the far end of the room, Elden Hinderschott stood quietly against the back wall, his expression unreadable among the restless crowd.

Dylan pushed off the bar and raised his voice, cutting through the low murmur of conversation.

"Okay, folks. Daylight's wastin', so we best get started. All of you are here 'cause you want to know if the rumors are true."

He let the silence settle, then nodded once.

"I can assure you they are. The Devil of Black Hills is alive."

A ripple of murmurs ran through the room—some men nodded grimly, others grinned like they'd just been handed a loaded gun.

Dylan continued, voice steady. "He killed our town's beloved pastor and his lovely wife in cold blood."

Elden watched the men shift restlessly, some clenching fists, others exchanging glances. The mood in the bar thickened, a mix of anger and anticipation.

"And I intend to make sure he pays for those crimes."

He paused, letting the words hang.

"Now do not underestimate this man. You've all heard the stories. You know what he's capable of. If you get a chance to take him down, you do not hesitate."

A burly bounty hunter near the front spoke up, voice booming.

"Just tell me two things, Sheriff."

All eyes turned to him.

"Where do I find him? And where do I collect the reward?"

Laughter erupted, sharp and rough. Someone clapped the burly man on the back.

Dylan nodded, smiling thinly, then stepped forward.

"That's funny. Real funny." His smile faded into something colder. "But that Devil already killed five of my men when they tried to take him in. So if jokes is all you got, I'll go ahead and have a pine box made for you, too."

The laughter died as though someone had snuffed a candle.

"Now...as far as where to find him, last we heard—"

The barroom doors slammed open. The wagon driver burst in, coat flapping, face pale and breathless.

"Sheriff!"

Dylan straightened.

***

Outside Skinny's, a covered wagon sat in the middle of the street, horses stamping nervously. Dylan threw back the blanket in the wagon bed, revealing the Rousey family's bodies piled one atop the other, blood-soaked and broken, faces frozen in the last moments of shock and pain.

The bounty hunters who had spilled out from Skinny's gasped and muttered. Some stepped back, others leaned in, wide-eyed. The burly man from earlier pushed through the crowd, took one look, and turned away to vomit into the dirt.

Dylan stared down at the bodies, jaw tight. "What happened?"

The driver wiped his mouth with a trembling hand. "Found 'em on the way here. Just as that Devil was high-tailin' it out."

Dylan's eyes swept over the corpses—the rope burns on Hank's neck, the bullet holes in Kurt's chest and head, the mangled ruin of Len Sr.'s body. He covered them again with the blanket, then turned to the crowd.

"I hope this makes clear what we're dealin' with. Now, on top of the reward, I've got a hundred-dollar bill for any man who'll help me hunt down the Devil of Black Hills."

The crowd nodded, but the enthusiasm had dimmed. Faces were pale, eyes uncertain. Prichard shook his head slightly and leaned in close to Dylan.

"Just how many men you tryin' to get killed? We don't need them. I can take the Devil down myself."

Dylan kept his voice low. "You'll get your chance. Just make sure our clients are ready to pay."

He turned to the driver, louder. "Where'd you say you found 'em?"

"East of town, about ten miles."

"And which way was he headed?"

"Took off to the northwest."

Prichard shook his head again. "He's circlin' back? Why?"

"Tryin' to throw us off," Dylan said. "Probably head back east after a few miles."

A voice called from the crowd. "Sheriff?"

Heads turned. A scrawny man had his hand raised, eyes bright with nervous excitement. Elden watched from the porch of the bar, arms folded.

The scrawny man swallowed. "It's a long shot. But I got an idea of where he might be goin'."

Maggie

THE FOREST HAD GROWN denser as they rode, the pines closing in like silent sentinels, their branches heavy with late-winter snow that dripped in slow, steady plinks onto the frozen ground below. The horse moved at a careful walk, hooves crunching softly over the thin crust of ice and needles. Wakan sat in front, her small frame straight and alert, while the Devil rode behind her, his arms reaching around to hold the reins loosely in his gloved hands. The warmth of his chest pressed against her back, a steady presence that kept the biting wind from cutting too deep.

She shifted slightly in the saddle, glancing up at the narrow path ahead where sunlight filtered in thin shafts through the canopy.

"How much further?" she asked, her voice carrying a mix of weariness and quiet curiosity.

The Devil guided the horse around a low-hanging branch, his breath warm against her ear. "We're gittin' close to her cabin."

Wakan turned her head just enough to see the side of his face, the scar around his neck catching a fleeting glint of light. "Her? Does she know who you are? What you've done?"

He didn't answer right away, just adjusted the reins to steer them past a cluster of boulders half-buried in snow.

"She does," he said finally, his tone even, almost matter-of-fact.

Wakan considered that, her fingers tightening on the saddle horn. "And she's not afraid of you?"

The Devil chuckled then, a low, rough sound that rumbled through his chest and into her back. "Doubt she's afraid of anybody."

The horse plodded on, the only sounds the creak of leather, the soft snort of breath from the animal, and the distant call of a raven high overhead. Wakan glanced at the trees passing slowly by, their trunks dark and straight against the white ground.

"So why hasn't she ever turned you in and collected the bounty?"

He shrugged, the motion shifting the saddle beneath them. "Don't know. But she could've. She's a tough ol' broad."

A sharp voice cut through the quiet from somewhere behind the thick brush to their left. "Who you callin' old?"

The Devil pulled the reins gently but firmly, bringing the horse to a halt. At the unmistakable metallic click of a rifle hammer being cocked back, he raised his hands slowly from the reins, palms open.

"Easy Maggie," he said calmly, "it's just me."

From the bushes stepped an old woman, wiry and weathered, her face a map etched by decades of hard living under open skies. Her gray hair was pulled back in a practical knot beneath a faded wool cap, and she held an old Winchester steady, though her eyes were sharp and knowing rather than fearful.

"I ain't worried about you," she said, her voice gravelly but strong. "Who's with you?"

Wakan leaned out from behind the Devil's broad frame, peering around him with a tentative smile.

"Hi."

Maggie's gaze shifted to the girl, taking in her young face, the braids, the curious eyes. After a moment, the tension eased from her shoulders, and she lowered the rifle, the barrel dipping slowly toward the ground. There may have been a sense of shock on Maggie's face.

"Hi yourself."

***

The rustic cabin sat nestled in a small clearing, its logs darkened by smoke and years, the roof sagging slightly under a blanket of pine needles and lingering snow. Just down a gentle embankment, a narrow river rushed clear and cold over smooth stones, its steady murmur filling the air like a constant whisper. Furs of various sizes—wolf, beaver, deer—hung stretched between the trees on rawhide lines, tanning slowly in the crisp daylight, their edges fluttering faintly in the breeze that carried the sharp scent of wet earth and curing hides.

Wakan stood near a rough-hewn trough by the cabin wall, patting the horse's strong neck as it dipped its muzzle into the water, drinking deeply with soft, contented snorts. Steam rose faintly from its flanks in the cool air. A little ways off, Maggie and the Devil stood talking, their voices low against the river's song.

"So this girl...Wakan?" Maggie asked, glancing toward the child with a thoughtful tilt of her head.

The Devil nodded. "Yeah. It's short for some other name ain't nobody got time to say."

Maggie offered a soft smile, the lines around her eyes deepening with genuine affection. "She came all this way alone to find her father?" she said softly. "Brave little girl."

The Devil glanced at Wakan, his expression a mix of respect and concern. "There's a thin line between brave and stupid. Lucky she's alive." He paused, shifting his weight. "You know I hate to trouble you with this, but we got nowhere else to go. I'm sure they'll have every road covered."

Maggie waved him off with a dismissive flick of her hand, the gesture firm but kind.

"Just need to hold up a few days," he added. "Let things die down."

Wakan finished patting the horse and walked toward them, her steps light on the packed earth, curiosity bright in her eyes.

"No trouble at all," Maggie said warmly, just as Wakan reached them.

Wakan looked up at the older woman, taking in the cabin, the furs, the river beyond. "You're a trapper, too? Like him?"

Maggie's smile widened. "Oh, I'm better than him."

She slipped a strong, callused arm around Wakan's shoulders and gently led her toward the cabin door, the girl falling into step beside her without hesitation.

"I taught him everything he knows," Maggie added with a wink over her shoulder.

The Devil smiled faintly and shook his head as the two walked ahead, Maggie's arm steady around the child. He followed behind, ready to cross the threshold into the welcoming warmth of the cabin.

But before he could, Maggie's hand planted firmly on his chest, stopping him cold.

"Where you going?" she asked, eyebrow arched.

He looked down at her hand, then at the open door. "Inside. Been ridin' half the day. I'd like to sit down."

"Yeah?" Maggie's tone was matter-of-fact. "Well, you smell like death. There's some soap over there." She nodded toward a rough bar of lye soap sitting on the porch railing. "Go to the river and clean up. Scrub your clothes, too. We'll hang 'em by the fire inside."

The Devil's shoulders sagged.

Maggie turned her attention back to Wakan, guiding her fully inside. "As for you, young lady, we'll draw you a nice, warm bath, and I might just have some old clothes that belonged to my daughter and will fit you just fine."

As the door began to swing shut, the Devil called after them, half-pleading. "Well...why can't I get a warm bath?"

The door closed firmly in his face with a solid thunk. He stood there a moment, staring at the weathered wood, then sighed deeply. He scooped up the bar of soap from the railing, tucked it into his pocket, and turned toward the river, boots crunching down the embankment as the water's rush grew louder.

Preparations

T HE TOWN SQUARE OF Buffalo Ridge hummed with restless energy as evening settled over the Dakota Territory, the last streaks of sunset bleeding orange across the snow-dusted rooftops. Lanterns flickered to life in windows, casting warm pools of light on the muddy streets where bounty hunters and townsfolk bustled like ants stirred by a boot. Men in heavy coats and wide-brimmed hats loaded saddlebags with ammunition, jerky, and bedrolls, their voices rising in gruff laughter and boasts. Horses stamped and snorted at hitching posts, their breath fogging the chill air, while women hurried children indoors, casting wary glances at the armed strangers who had flooded the town. The air carried the sharp scent of gun oil, horse sweat, and woodsmoke from hastily lit stoves.

Elden Hinderschott stood on the stoop of his general store, broom in hand, sweeping away the day's accumulation of dirt and pine needles. The rhythmic swish of bristles was a steady counterpoint to the chaos unfolding around him. He paused occasionally to watch the scene: a group of hunters arguing over a map by lantern light, another sharpening knives with the scrape of whetstone on steel. His eyes lingered on the faces—hard men with scarred hands and colder stares, drawn here by the promise of gold and glory.

Across the street, Sheriff Dylan strode through the center of the thoroughfare like a man conducting an orchestra, raising a hand to redirect a rider, barking orders to another group trying to hitch a mule team. His coat was open, badge glinting, voice carrying over the general murmur.

"Hey!" Dylan called, pointing at a covered wagon being loaded with crates and bedrolls. "You ain't takin' that wagon!"

The driver—a wiry man with a red scarf knotted at his throat—turned, hands spread in question. "Why?"

"Ain't gonna be no roads where we're goin'!" Dylan answered, walking closer. "Horses only!"

The driver shrugged, resigned, and started unhitching the team. Elden leaned on his broom, watching. "Hey, Sheriff!"

Dylan turned, his expression tight with the weight of the evening's preparations.

"You have a minute?"

Dylan glanced around at the milling crowd, the horses being saddled, the men checking their rifles. "I think you can see I don't."

Elden straightened, undeterred. "Well, if there's anything you need—"

"I got everything covered," Dylan cut in, already turning away. "Thank you, though."

Elden nodded, but his eyes stayed sharp as Prichard approached from the shadows of a nearby alley, his steps purposeful. Elden eased back against a porch post, sweeping slowly now, positioning himself to overhear without drawing notice.

Prichard leaned in close to Dylan. "A group of our clients will meet us just over the ridge. Another group's gonna meet us there."

Elden's broom paused mid-sweep, his ear tuned to their low voices amid the square's clamor.

"They know the way?" Dylan asked.

"Billy's with 'em. He says he knows."

"And they know to hang back until we get there?"

"Yeah. That won't be a problem." Prichard paused, then added, "What about the guys out at the pastor's place?"

Elden's curiosity sharpened; he swept a little closer, pretending to clear a stubborn clump of dirt.

Dylan shook his head. "Nah. I think we have all the manpower we need. Let 'em keep lookin'."

Prichard nodded once and walked off, melting back into the crowd. Elden resumed sweeping with steady strokes, but as Dylan turned, their eyes met for a brief moment. Dylan's gaze narrowed suspiciously, lingering a beat too long before he looked away and continued down the street, barking orders at another group saddling horses.

Elden watched him go, broom moving slower now, his mind turning over the fragments of conversation he'd caught—the clients, the ridge, the men at the pastor's place. The square bustled on around him, but he stood there a moment longer, the broom forgotten in his hands.

The Deepest Scars

THE RIVER DOWN THE embankment caught the last light of the sun as it dipped low behind the pines. The river's surface shimmering like polished metal as it rushed steadily over the rocks. Wakan sat on the edge of the porch, legs swinging gently, admiring the simple dress Maggie had found for her—soft wool, faded but clean, fitting her small frame far better than the travel-worn clothes she had arrived in. She smoothed the fabric over her knees, then turned her gaze to the river below.

The Devil stood waist-deep in the cold water, shirtless, holding his pants up with one hand while scrubbing them vigorously with the bar of soap in the other. Water streamed down his arms and chest as he worked. He rose slightly higher, the river lapping at his waist, revealing his back—a map of old violence: long scars from knives and whips, puckered burns from fire or branding irons, and the pale, healed circles of bullet wounds scattered across his skin like cruel constellations. Wakan's breath caught in her throat; she stared for a frozen moment, then quickly looked away, cheeks warming.

Maggie's voice came soft from the doorway behind her. "They say the deepest scars are the ones you can't see."

Wakan glanced up at the older woman, then dropped her eyes to the porch boards, tracing the grain with her finger.

"Have you known him long?" she asked quietly.

Maggie lowered herself onto the step beside her, the wood creaking under her weight. "Long enough to have dressed many of those wounds. When I found him, there was little left of what anyone could call a man. He didn't trust anyone or anything. He's come a long ways."

Wakan watched as the Devil submerged again, rinsing the soap from his clothes.

"Do you know his name?"

Maggie shook her head slowly. "Trust will only get you so far with him, I'm afraid."

Wakan's gaze drifted back to the river, where the Devil now stood fully submerged to his shoulders, scrubbing at his hair.

"There's this old story," Maggie continued, voice low and thoughtful, "that evil demons walk among us, wreaking havoc and spreading misery everywhere they go. But some believe that if you can call one of these demons by its name, you can control it. Tame it somehow."

Wakan turned to look at her.

"I think..." Maggie said, eyes on the river, "that man out there doesn't quite know what he is. Or maybe he's afraid of what he means to this world." She paused, then added, "Now I don't think he believes that story about the demons. But he makes sure no one can call him by his name. Just in case."

Maggie slapped Wakan lightly on the knee, the sound sharp in the quiet evening. "Come on inside. You can help me make dinner."

***

Inside Maggie's cabin, night had fully fallen, the windows glowing warm from the fire in the hearth and the lantern on the table. The three of them sat around the rough kitchen table finishing supper—Wakan on the same side as the Devil, her plate nearly clean again. The air smelled of roasted meat, boiled potatoes, and fresh bread.

The Devil pushed his empty plate away and leaned back in his chair, patting his stomach with satisfaction.

"Shit, Maggie! You always could make up a good spread."

Maggie shot him a stern look. "Hey, watch your language."

She glanced at Wakan and shook her head in mock exasperation. Wakan laughed, the sound bright and unexpected in the small room.

"Well," Maggie said, smiling at the girl, "this house hasn't heard the laugh of a child in some time. It'll do its old bones good."

She looked at Wakan's plate. "Do you want more?"

Wakan nodded vigorously. Maggie scooped another generous portion onto her plate.

The Devil watched with a faint grin. "Watch out, now. She's small, but she'll eat your house clean to those bones if you let her."

Both Maggie and Wakan laughed again, the sound filling the cabin like sunlight.

"There's plenty to go around," Maggie said as she sat back down.

She leaned her elbows on the table, looking between them. "So...you stay here a few days. Then what?"

The Devil shrugged. "I dunno. Make sure she gets home."

He glanced at Wakan. "After that, maybe find those papers the pastor gave you."

He turned to Maggie. "Maybe you can help there."

He sat up straighter, using his hands as he spoke, gesturing toward the table and Maggie. "No one's lookin' for you, right? Wakan here says she hid these papers, whatever they are, in some hollow tree near that pastor's cabin."

Wakan quietly removed her headdress and began digging around the inner brim. Maggie watched her curiously as the Devil continued.

"So I figure while I get her home, you could go down there and see what you can find. Maybe Wakan makes a map or somethin'. Tells you what sorta landmarks might have been around this tree that will help you—"

He looked up to see Maggie staring at him, a knowing grin on her face.

"What?"

She nodded toward Wakan.

He turned. Wakan held folded papers out to him, her expression steady.

He stared at them a long moment, then looked at Wakan.

"Had to make sure I could trust you," she said quietly.

Slowly, the Devil reached out and took the papers. He unfolded them carefully and pulled the candle closer, leaning the pages toward the light.

Maggie leaned in. "What is it?"

The Devil's eyes scanned the lines. "It's...a list of names. Clients of the sheriff."

He shuffled to the next page.

Maggie frowned. "Clients? For what?"

"For hunts," he said, voice hardening. "The sheriff is kidnapping Lakota for them to hunt."

Silence fell heavy over the table. Wakan's eyes went wide, welling with tears.

"My father!"

Maggie reached across and grabbed her hand, squeezing it tight.

The Devil shuffled the pages again. "There's another page."

Maggie's voice was gentle. "Perhaps that's enough for tonight."

Through tears, Wakan asked, "What is it?"

The Devil took a deep breath, jaw clenched. "It's another client list."

He gritted his teeth. "The ones who'll pay extra to hunt children."

***

Later that night, the cabin had grown quiet, the fire burned low in the hearth. The Devil sat alone at the table, the papers still in his hand, but his gaze fixed blankly out the window into the dark. The candle flickered, casting long shadows across the walls.

He heard Wakan chuckling softly and turned toward Maggie's open bedroom door, where Maggie was tucking the girl into bed, her gentle teasing drawing laughter from the child.

The Devil looked back at the pages in his hand, lost in thought.

Maggie's voice came from the doorway. "You should go tuck her in."

He looked at her, puzzled. "I should...what now?"

As she crossed the room and settled into a chair, "You know. Tuck her in. Tell her good night."

He shook his head. "Why? I ain't never done nothin' like that in my life."

She smiled faintly. "Which is why you should do it now. Go on. It'll be good for your soul."

***

In Maggie's bedroom moments later, Wakan lay staring at the ceiling beams, the quilt pulled up to her chin. The Devil cleared his throat from the doorway. She turned her head and saw his head just barely peeking in.

Then he stepped fully into the doorway, hands in his pockets.

He took one hand out and gave her an awkward wave. "Good night, then."

He started to leave.

"Hey," Wakan called softly.

He came back.

"Why does he do it? The Sheriff?"

The Devil stared at her a moment. "Money. Only reason there could be."

He paused. "Get some sleep."

He started to walk away again.

"Do you think my father was one of the people they...hunted?"

The Devil stared at her longer, then sighed. This time he stepped fully into the room and approached her bed.

"Probably so," he said quietly. "I'm sorry."

Wakan's voice trembled. "Do you think he...was scared?"

The Devil took a seat in the chair beside the bed. "Probably, yes. Any man would be."

"Including you?"

He nodded. "Including me."

Wakan looked down, tears slipping silently as she sobbed.

The Devil leaned forward slightly. "But you know what I bet...given what I know of you? I bet he fought 'em. I bet they ain't never had a tougher hunt. Wouldn't doubt it if some of 'em didn't make it out alive."

He paused. "Yeah. Your daddy...I bet he gave 'em hell."

She looked up at him through her tears and managed a small smile.

The Devil stood to leave.

"Hey," she called one last time.

He turned just inside the doorway, hand on the knob.

"I asked her, you know. Maggie. I asked her why she never turned you in. Why she never reaped any reward from you."

The Devil glanced toward Maggie in the other room. Now she was the one studying the pages Wakan had given him. He turned back to Wakan.

"Yeah? And what'd she say?"

With tears still in her eyes, Wakan whispered, "She said she already had."

The Devil stared at her for a long moment. Then he pulled the door closed softly behind him.

A Law Matter

THE BACKROOM OF HINDERSCHOTT'S General Store felt smaller than usual, the walls pressing in with the weight of stacked crates and shadowed shelves. The single lantern on the desk cast a feeble circle of light, leaving the corners swallowed in darkness. Elden sat hunched over the open ledger, pencil gripped tightly in his hand, but the neat columns of figures blurred before his eyes. He wasn't seeing numbers—he was hearing fragments of overheard conversations that refused to settle into anything harmless.

A soft hand settled on his shoulder.

Elden flinched hard, the chair legs scraping sharply against the floorboards.

Eleanor's quiet laugh broke the silence. "I'm sorry. I'm sorry."

He pressed a hand to his chest, breathing out slowly, rubbing at eyes that felt grainy with fatigue and something heavier.

"You've been stuck in here most of the evening," she said, her voice gentle but edged with worry. "You comin' upstairs anytime soon?"

He leaned back, the chair creaking, and stared at the low ceiling beams as if answers might be written there.

"Yeah, I...uh..."

The pause stretched, thick and uncomfortable.

"No. No, there's something I need to go do. But I won't be long."

He stood abruptly, kissed her cheek—a quick, distracted brush of lips—then reached for his hat. Eleanor watched him, perplexity deepening the lines around her eyes.

"Elden...it's already so late."

"I know." His voice was quiet, almost apologetic, but resolute. "I just...need to check on something."

***

Outside, the night air bit sharp and cold, the kind that crept under collars and made horses blow steam. Elden rode at a careful trot down the narrow path toward the Josephs' place, the horse's hooves muffled on the frozen trail. The forest pressed close on both sides, black trunks rising into a starless sky. But the woods were not silent. Far from it.

Torchlight flickered ahead—at least a dozen small, bobbing flames moving along the inner edges of the trees like will-o'-the-wisps. Men's voices carried faintly on the wind, low and purposeful, punctuated by the occasional shout or the crack of a branch under boot. Through the skeletal branches deeper in, more torches glowed, weaving methodical patterns as the search parties combed the underbrush. The scene felt like a slow, deliberate encirclement.

Elden slowed his horse further, eyes narrowing as he took in the scale of it—the quiet intensity, the sheer number of men fanning out among the wilderness.

A voice cut through the dark from the old fence line. "Mister Hinderschott? Can I help you with somethin'?"

Elden turned to see Ralph Gosling step from the shadows, rifle cradled in his arms, his silhouette bulky against the faint glow of a distant torch. Elden pulled his horse to a full stop as Ralph approached, boots crunching on the frost.

"I just...uh..."

Elden's gaze drifted toward the barn, its doors hanging open, a faint whinny drifting from within.

"Wanted to check on the Josephs' horses. Make sure they were fed and watered until the sheriff can figure out what to do with them."

Ralph followed his look toward the barn, then turned back, expression unreadable in the low light.

"I'll make sure of it."

Elden nodded slowly, but his eyes swept the surrounding activity once more—the torches gliding deeper into the woods, the men's shadows stretching long and strange across the snow.

"So...what's going on?" he asked, keeping his tone casual. "I wasn't expecting anyone to be here."

Ralph shifted the rifle slightly, the movement deliberate. "That's a...law matter. Nothin' for you to worry about."

The pause that followed felt heavier than the cold.

"Now," Ralph added, voice firm, "why don't you head on home and let us do our jobs."

Elden held his gaze a moment longer, then nodded again, turning the horse slowly. As he started back down the path, he glanced once more over his shoulder. The torches continued their slow, relentless dance through the trees, the light flickering like restless spirits that refused to let the night—or the secrets it held—rest.

Not Coming Back

THE SOUNDS BEGAN AS usual—low, guttural choking, ragged and desperate, as if a noose were tightening inch by inch. Gunshots cracked sharp and sudden, echoing in the dark. The vicious snap of a bullwhip cut through the air, followed by more choking, wet and labored. Sinister laughter rose, low and mocking, layered over the screams of women and children—high, piercing, filled with terror. Another snap of the whip, cruel and precise. The choking grew louder, frantic. The laughter swelled, crueler still. Another vicious snap of the whip.

The Devil jolted awake on his cot, eyes wide in the dim glow of the banked fire. His chest heaved, hand clutching at his heart as if to still its frantic pounding. Sweat beaded on his brow despite the chill. For a long moment he sat there, legs swinging slowly off the cot to the cold floorboards, staring down at the shadows between his bare feet, breath coming in shallow, uneven pulls.

His gaze drifted to his gun belt hanging from the footpost, the silver barrels catching the faint ember light like accusing eyes.

***

Uutside the cabin, the night air was sharp and still, the river's murmur the only sound under a sky thick with stars. The Devil worked quickly in the dark, saddling the horse with practiced, silent movements, his back to the cabin door. He shoved the folded papers deep into a saddlebag, securing the flap with a tight tug. Then he lifted his gun belt, buckling it around his waist with deliberate care.

Maggie's footsteps approached soft on the frozen ground behind him.

"There's a guy in town," he said without turning, voice low. "If I get the papers to him, he'll know what to do with them."

"And you can trust him?"

He paused, tightening a strap. "Trust him not to shoot me? I don't know. Trust him to do the right thing by Wakan. Yeah. I think so."

He glanced toward the eastern horizon, where the first hint of gray was beginning to bruise the sky. "He owns the grocery store in town. I think I can get there just before he opens up."

"Did you tell Wakan you're going?"

"Of course not." He kept working, voice steady but edged. "She'd want to come along. Safer if she stays here."

Maggie stepped closer. "Then you didn't tell her you're not coming back."

He stopped, hands still on the belt, and exhaled slowly, the breath clouding in the cold.

"I know you didn't sleep," she said quietly. "I could hear you. You're having the dreams again."

He resumed buckling, tighter now. "You're assuming they ever stopped."

She reached out, her hand barely brushing his shoulder. He pulled away sharply, focusing on the leather strap as if it required all his attention.

"She needs you to get her home."

"You know the way there just as well as I do."

"You have to keep her safe."

"You can do that better than me."

"They are looking for her."

He turned on her suddenly, voice rising in the still night, eyes fierce.

"They are looking for her, but they are HUNTING ME! Do you understand that? You want her to stay alive? This is the best thing for her!"

He paused, chest rising and falling, the words hanging heavy between them.

"Because the next time some bounty hunter lines me up in his sights...the LAST place you want her... is standing next to me."

He looked down at his hips, at the grotesque guns hanging there, the etched skulls seeming to leer in the faint starlight. Slowly, he drew them, the silver catching the dim glow, and held them out to her.

"Here. Take these. I don't need 'em anymore."

Maggie took them, the weight heavy in her hands.

"And what should I do with 'em?"

He shook his head, eyes distant. "Whatever you want. Those guns...what they stand for...I want no part of it. Not anymore. Toss 'em in the river. Melt 'em down. I don't care."

He climbed into the saddle, settling with a creak of leather.

"For my part," he said, gathering the reins, "I'll try and find out where the sheriff's looking for us. See if I can lure them away from here."

He looked at her one last time. "Take care of her, Maggie," he said. "Get her home."

He snapped the reins and trotted away into the darkness, the sound of hooves fading slowly until the sounds of the racing river were all that remained.

Meeting with the Devil

E LDEN STOOD BEHIND THE counter of his general store, setting down a wooden crate of canned goods and dry staples with a soft thud. The store smelled of coffee grounds, lamp oil, and the faint sweetness of fresh bread from the bakery next door.

"Sam..." he called, voice low but carrying.

Samantha skipped lightly from the aisle, braids bouncing. "Yes, sir?"

"Take these and put them on the shelves, please."

She grabbed the crate with both arms, grunting slightly under the weight. "Yes, sir."

Elden watched her go, then added, "And don't forget. Those go behind the ones that are already there."

"Yes, sir, rotate the stock. I know," came her voice from the back aisle, cheerful and obedient.

Elden smiled to himself, then added, "And be quick about it, okay. We open in ten minutes."

A faint creak sounded from the open backroom door. Elden's eyes snapped toward it. A shadow shifted—just a flicker—in the dimness beyond.

Keeping his gaze fixed on the aisle where Samantha worked, humming softly to herself, Elden's hand moved slowly beneath the counter. His fingers closed around the grip of a pistol, the wood cool and familiar against his palm. He drew it inch by inch, heart beginning to thud hard against his ribs.

He stepped quietly around the counter and into the narrow hallway leading to the backroom, gun raised, barrel steady despite the sudden tightness in his chest. The darkness there felt thicker, the air heavier. He reached the semi-closed office door, breath shallow, and shoved it open with his boot, swinging the pistol in a quick arc.

The small office was empty—only his desk, the lantern still burning low from the night before, papers scattered where he had left them.

Cold metal pressed against his cheek.

Elden froze as the Devil's hand slid into place around his gun, firm and unyielding, and pulled it gingerly from his own.

The Devil's voice came low from behind him. "Sit down."

Elden took a cautious step forward. A hard shove between his shoulder blades sent him stumbling into the office chair. He sat heavily.

The Devil stepped into the room, closing the door softly behind him with a click that sounded unnaturally loud in the silence.

"Do you know who I am?"

Elden nodded slowly, eyes never leaving the silver revolver pointed at his face.

"Then you know what I can do."

Elden said nothing, throat dry.

"I ain't kilt the pastor and his wife." He waited for Elden's protest. It never came. "Do you believe me?"

Elden hesitated, gaze flicking to the gun, then back to the scarred face in the shadows.

"There's men out at their cabin. They're searching the woods around it," he said finally, voice steady despite the tension. "What are they lookin' for?"

The Devil lowered the pistol slightly, dug into his front pocket, and tossed the folded papers onto the desk. They landed with a soft slap.

Elden glanced down, then picked them up, unfolding them carefully under the lantern's glow.

"What is it?"

"It's proof of the sheriff's illegal doin's. And everyone who's involved."

Elden scanned the pages, eyes widening as familiar names leaped out at him.

"Jesus," he whispered. "I know all these people. Hell, half of 'em went to the pastor's church."

"And that there's the pastor's handwritin'," the Devil said quietly. "It's why he's dead."

"Daddy..." Samantha's voice drifted from the hallway, bright and innocent.

The Devil's eyes flicked to the door. He pressed himself flat against the wall as the door opened, hiding him.

"I finished stocking the shelves," Samatha said. "Do you want me to go ahead and open up?"

Elden's eyes tracked briefly over to the Devil behind the door and his pistol pointed at Sam through it. Elden stood quickly and moved to her.

"Oh...No. No," he called, forcing calm into his voice. "I'll do that in a few minutes. Why don't you go upstairs and see if your mother needs anything."

"You sure?"

Elden eased her back, hand gentle on her shoulder, guiding her away from the door and toward the hall. "I'm sure. Just finishing up some things in here."

"Okay," she said, footsteps receding. "Hey. We're low on rice."

"Okay. Okay, I'll write that down. Thank you."

He closed the door softly, leaned against it for a heartbeat, then turned. The Devil lowered the gun, eyes steady on him.

Elden lifted the papers. "So this got the pastor and his wife killed. And you want to give it to me? Why not just kill me yourself and save the sheriff the trouble."

"The mistake the pastor made was not telling anyone. Trying to keep it to himself." The Devil's voice was low, urgent. "I want you to tell everyone. Show this to anyone you see. Spread the word."

He brushed past Elden and into the hallway.

"And in about three days," he continued, "go to the Lakota reservation. There'll be a little girl there who can testify that the sheriff had the Josephs killed. She witnessed it."

"Wait. What?" Elden followed a step. "Lakota reservation? Little girl? And just where will you be while I'm risking my life and the lives of my wife and daughter?"

The Devil opened the chamber of Elden's pistol, letting the bullets clatter to the floor one by one.

"I'm gonna go find a rock. And crawl under it for another fifteen years."

He tossed the empty weapon into Elden's chest. Elden caught it reflexively.

"But one more thing..."

"Yeah?" Elden's voice carried a bitter edge. "Is that all? Just one more?"

"Tell me where the sheriff and his posse's huntin' for me."

"Why? So you can avoid 'em?" Elden's eyes narrowed. "Well, how do you know I won't just send you right to 'em?"

The Devil pointed to the papers still clutched in Elden's hand. "You wouldn't have those if I didn't think I could trust you."

Elden looked down at the pages, sighed heavily.

"They said they were headin' southeast."

The Devil nodded, tipping his hat slightly. "Much obliged."

He started down the hallway, then paused, turning back.

"Southeast? Why southeast?"

Elden shook his head slowly. "This bounty hunter got this crazy notion. Since you were fur trappin'...well, there's this other fur trapper...this old lady...lives out that way. Margaret? Martha?"

"Maggie."

Realization dawned on Elden's face, sharp and sudden.

"I'm coming with you!" He stooped quickly, scooping up the scattered bullets.

The Devil was already moving, running down the hallway.

"No! Do what I told you to do! Tell everyone about Dylan!"

The back door of the store swung open hard, banging against the wall. The Devil burst out into the pale morning light, vaulting onto his horse in one fluid motion. He whipped the reins sharply, and the animal surged forward, hooves thundering on the frozen ground as he galloped away from the store, disappearing down the alley in a swirl of dust.

Tomorrow Will Never Come

THE DEVIL SLOWED HIS horse as Maggie's cabin came into view through the thinning trees, the familiar sight now twisted into something wrong. He slid from the saddle in one quiet motion, boots hitting the ground without a sound, and drew a pistol. He approached the cabin from the side, every sense straining against the unnatural stillness.

Some of the furs that had hung stretched between the trees now lay trampled on the ground, their raw edges muddied and torn. A window in the cabin wall stared back at him with broken panes, jagged glass glinting like teeth in the dim afternoon.

"Maggie?" he called, voice low, edged with a dread he couldn't quite name.

He glanced down the embankment to the river, its rush steady and indifferent. Nothing moved there—no figure washing clothes, no familiar silhouette against the water.

"Wakan?"

No answer came, only the wind stirring the fallen furs.

He turned the corner to the front of the cabin, gun raised. A dead man lay sprawled across the porch, blood pooled thick and dark beneath him, eyes staring blankly at the sky.

The Devil strode up the steps, the pistol now held tight to his chest, back pressed to the cabin wall beside the door. He took a slow breath, then swung inside, gun at the ready.

The door opened only halfway, catching on something heavy. He peered around it—a second body blocked the way, slumped against the frame. He pushed his way in.

The room was a wreck: furniture toppled and splintered, chairs overturned, dishes shattered across the floorboards. The air smelled of gunpowder and blood, sharp and metallic.

"Maggie? Wakan?"

A faint moan rose from the chaos. The Devil's eyes snapped to the overturned kitchen table, where Maggie's legs extended from beneath it, one boot twitching weakly.

He ran over, holstered his pistol, and tossed the table aside with a crash. Maggie lay on her stomach, fingers scraping feebly at the floor as she tried to move.

He turned her over gently. Blood spurted from a wound in her abdomen, soaking her shirt dark and spreading fast across the wood beneath her.

"Okay. Okay, I got you," he assured her.

He felt around her back frantically—no exit wound. She grimaced, face pale and slick with sweat.

"Okay. Let's get you down to the river. Clean you up. Then—"

"I'm sorry," she rasped, voice thin.

He shook his head fiercely. "Ain't nothing to be sorry about. We'll clean you up and see about gettin' that bullet out of you."

She shook her head, weaker now. "Ain't no frettin' over the bullet."

"Hush now. We just gotta..."

He looked around desperately, eyes wild, then snatched up a dishrag from the floor and pressed it hard into the wound. Maggie grimaced, a sharp gasp escaping her lips.

"Just gotta stop this bleedin'. Then we're gonna get to that bullet."

She shook her head again, grabbing weakly at his arm. "You know ain't no use—"

"Quiet now!" His voice cracked. "We just gotta clean you up! You're doin' good!"

She pulled at his sleeve, fingers trembling as she tried to reach his face.

"Hey... hey..." she whispered.

Tears welled in his eyes, blurring his vision as he fought the panic rising in his chest.

"We'll git you to town. There's a doctor there that—"

Her bloodied hand found his cheek, smearing it red, then slid to the back of his neck, pulling him down until their eyes met.

"Hey!" she said, voice firm despite the pain. "Save the girl! Save Wakan."

A tear tumbled down his cheek as he stared into her fading eyes.

"Where is she, Maggie? Where'd they take her?"

"Hey, Devil!" Sheriff Dylan's voice boomed from outside, sharp and biting.

The Devil held his breath. Maggie closed her eyes, a final acceptance settling over her features.

"That you in there?"

The Devil laid Maggie down slowly, gently, pulling a crumpled tablecloth over for a pillow beneath her head. She grasped his hand weakly as he stood. He looked down at her; she shook her head, slow and certain.

Outside, Dylan stood in the clearing, Prichard a few paces away, the sheriff's hand clamped firm around Wakan's wrist. She twisted fruitlessly, small struggles against his iron grip.

Dozens of men emerged from the woods on all sides—bounty hunters, clients, rifles and pistols glinting—encircling the cabin in a tightening ring of steel and intent.

The Devil peered carefully through the corner of a window, lifting the curtain just enough. He saw Dylan holding Wakan captive. His head dropped, shoulders sagging under the weight of it.

"You know," Dylan called, voice carrying clear and taunting, "as we were leavin', Prichard here thought he saw someone up on the ridge ridin' fast this way. I didn't think it could be you." He waited a moment. Looked around. "I mean, I told him you wouldn't be stupid enough to come back."

The Devil's voice rang out from inside, bitter. "Joke's on you, Dylan. I am that stupid!"

He looked down, shaking his head. Maggie stared up at him from the floor, her breathing shallow.

Dylan glanced at Prichard curiously; Prichard could only shrug. Dylan's eyes landed on the Devil's gun belt slung over Prichard's shoulder.

"Oh! Thanks for the guns, by the way!" Dylan called. "They are definitely one of a kind. Personally, I'd like to hang 'em on the wall of the sheriff's station. A sort of museum piece, you know. A little homage to the legendary Devil of Black Hills."

The Devil moved slowly around the cabin's interior, peering out various windows, assessing the situation. Everywhere he looked, bounty hunters stood ready, rifles raised, eyes fixed on the cabin.

"But I promised Prichard he could have 'em," Dylan continued. "Now, he has this thing, you see, where he likes to kill people with their own guns, and he'd hoped to kill you with these." A pause. "But... I don't think that's in the cards. Do you?"

He waited, expecting a reply that never came. "Besides, we can't quite figure out how to pull the triggers on 'em. They're locked somehow. Don't suppose you'd be willin' to share the secret..."

The Devil moved back to the window overlooking Dylan.

"How 'bout you put one of the guns to your head," he called, "and I'll tell you."

Dylan chuckled. "No. No, I don't think I'll do that." "Although... I really don't see any reason why you have to die today."

Prichard shot him a sharp look. Other men exchanged curious glances.

"I was just tellin' Prichard earlier," Dylan went on, "that a man like you...with your background..."

The Devil glanced down at Maggie. She inhaled shallowly, eyes fixed on the ceiling beams.

"With your...skills, as they are." Dylan looked around at the surrounding men. "You'd make a great fit on my team."

Prichard muttered quietly, "What are you doin'?"

Dylan waved him off.

"You wouldn't have to hide anymore," Dylan called. "Wouldn't have to always be looking over your shoulder. Wouldn't have to wonder where the bullet's gonna come from that ends your life or who's gonna fire it."

He waited again. Again, nothing.

"Now. How's that sound?"

The Devil's voice was flat. "Sounds like you talk a lot."

Dylan chuckled again. "I do. I do. People tell me that. But I mean what I say. And I'm a man of my word. And if any of what I just said sounds good to you...there's just one thing I ask..."

The Devil's eyes widened as Dylan yanked Wakan forward roughly, clearly hurting her.

"Just come out here," Dylan said, "and put a bullet in this girl's head."

The Devil's fist clenched tight at his side.

"You see, this girl here has caused me a bit of a fuss," Dylan continued. "The only reason she's still alive is because she tells me that she hid some information in the woods...information that wouldn't be good for me and others if it were to get out...and so, I've kept her alive so she can show me where it is."

Dylan looked down at Wakan and shook his head. "But the more I think about it, the more I think maybe she's lyin'. Maybe there is no evidence hidden in the woods. Maybe it died with the pastor and his wife." He waited. Then: "Or maybe this little girl gave it to you."

The Devil crouched below the window, back to the wall, gun raised.

"But none of that matters now," Dylan called. "Yeah, I know you killed a few of my men, and caused me some headaches yourself, but I'm willin' to let bygones be bygones."

Prichard shook his head.

"Just come out here...and kill this girl...and we'll wash our hands of the whole damn mess."

Wakan's face was pale with fear. The Devil looked down at Maggie. She gave him a slow, resolute nod. He closed his eyes, pressing his forehead briefly against the gun barrel as if in silent prayer.

"I'll come out there," the Devil called finally. "But you have to do one thing for me first."

Dylan smirked at Prichard. "Okay. Name it."

"Stand still."

Dylan stared at the cabin, puzzled.

Suddenly, the Devil rose and fired in a swift, precise motion. Dylan ducked just as the bullet whined past, taking a large chunk of his ear in a spray of blood, slamming instead into the chest of the bounty hunter standing behind him. The man dropped with a choked gasp.

Men dove for cover as Dylan and Prichard leaped behind trees, Dylan dragging Wakan with him. He clutched his bleeding ear, pain twisting his features. He looked around. Every eye was on h im.

"Well," he snarled, "don't just stand there! Kill the son-of-a-bi—"

Guns roared from all directions, a thunderous volley blanketing the cabin. Bullets tore through wood and glass, shattering what remained of the windows, splintering the doorframe.

The Devil dove to the floor, army-crawling across the splintered boards to Maggie as chunks of wood and shards of glass rained down around them. He covered her body with his own amid the deafening chaos.

Bounty hunters, clients, Prichard, Reilly, Dylan—everyone fired relentlessly, the air thick with smoke and the acrid bite of powder.

Eventually, Dylan raised a hand, motioning sharply. "Hold your fire! Hold your fire!"

The shooting ceased as suddenly as it had begun, leaving only the ring of echoes and the crackle of fresh damage.

The Devil leaned up cautiously, checking on Maggie. She shook her head weakly.

"Don't do that again."

"You alive in there, Devil?" Dylan called, voice laced with mockery. "I hope so, 'cause I want you to see somethin'!"

Dylan yanked Wakan forward again, hard enough to make her stumble, then pressed his pistol against her head. Blood oozed steadily down the side of his face from his ruined ear.

"I want you to watch while I kill this girl!"

The Devil scrambled low to the window, peering through a jagged hole.

"I want you to have a front-row seat to her brains decorating the grass."

"Don't you do it, Dylan!" the Devil screamed.

"I'm doin' it right now!"

"Leave her out of this! You wanna kill somebody! Come kill me!"

"Watch real close!"

"DON'T YOU DO IT!"

Dylan gritted his teeth, smiling cruelly as his finger tightened on the trigger.

"HEY!" a voice shouted from the crowd.

All eyes turned to Wilson, an aging short and paunchy client who held his rifle awkwardly, unsure.

"I thought there was supposed to be a hunt," Wilson said. "That's what I paid for, ain't it?"

The men glanced at one another. Some of the other clients nodded slowly.

"We were told we were hunting the Devil of Black Hills," Wilson continued, "but hell...this ain't been no kind of hunt. He practically gave himself up."

Dylan stared at him, pistol still against Wakan's head. "And just what do you propose we do?" he asked.

"Well, if we can't hunt the Devil..." Wilson pointed at Wakan. "Then we should hunt her."

More men nodded, murmurs rising.

"I mean," Wilson said, "I already paid my money. I'd like to get somethin' for it."

"Yeah!" others called. "That's right!" "I'd pay double to hunt her!"

Dylan, gun still pressed to Wakan's temple, looked to Prichard. Prichard shook his head.

Finally, Dylan shoved Wakan roughly into a bounty hunter's grasp, then snatched a crude Molotov cocktail from another man's hand.

The Devil exhaled in fleeting relief as Wakan remained unharmed for the moment. He sank to his knees before the window.

"You hear that, Devil?" Dylan shouted.

He struck a match, the flame flaring bright, and lit the rag stuffed in the liquor bottle.

"Tonight, we roast you like a turkey!"

He hurled the bottle. It shattered against the cabin roof, flames whooshing up in a hungry roar.

"And tomorrow," Dylan called over the crackle, "we hunt her like a dog!"

The Devil looked up at the ceiling, where smoke already curled and flames licked hungrily at the beams.

"You're not gonna see tomorrow, Dylan!" he roared back. "You hear me, you son-of-a-bitch! TOMORROW WILL NEVER COME!"

"LIGHT IT UP!" Dylan yelled.

The men cheered wildly as more bottles sailed through the air, smashing against the walls. Flames erupted everywhere, devouring the dry wood with terrifying speed.

At the same time, Dylan and the others opened fire again, bullets hammering the cabin from every angle.

The Devil dove flat as the barrage resumed, crawling swiftly to another window. A bounty hunter approached it, rearing back to throw another bottle. The Devil shot the bottle in his hand; it exploded in a bloom of fire, engulfing the man in flames as he screamed and staggered back.

Yet more bottles crashed through other windows, liquor and fire spreading rapidly. Flames leaped up the walls, heat rising fast, smoke choking the air.

The Devil crawled low to the back of the cabin, staying beneath the hail of bullets, and peered through a knothole in the wood. Two clients stood shooting between him and the barn beyond.

"Maggie!"

He crawled quickly to her side. "Maggie, I think there are only two of them in back. If you can hold a gun, we get to the barn—"

He turned her toward him. Her eyes stared blankly, a fresh bullet hole in her forehead, blood trickling down her temple. He gritted his teeth, a raw sound escaping his throat, and pulled her briefly to his chest in a fierce, silent embrace.

He laid her down gently, then crawled to the back door. Bullets whined overhead. He reached up, grasped the knob, then stood in a burst of motion and threw the door open.

The two clients turned, startled. He dropped one with a quick shot, but more men—clients and bounty hunters he hadn't seen—flanked the sides. Their bullets drove him back inside in a storm of splinters and lead.

He fell backward into the cabin, firing as he went, and kicked the door shut.

Above him, wood groaned and snapped. A section of the roof gave way with a roar, flames and burning beams crashing down.

The Devil crawled to the center of the room, pulled his weighted blade, and swung it hard at the floorboards. It cracked the wood. He swung again, widening a small hole.

He clawed at the planks, yanking them up desperately as the roof collapsed further around him, heat searing, smoke blinding. As beams fell in a thunderous cascade, he jumped into the shallow hole beneath the floor, reaching out to drag the upturned kitchen table over him like a shield just as the rest of the roof caved in.

Outside, the men cheered wildly. Dylan grinned wide, blood still dripping from his ear, as the cabin became an inferno.

Prichard shook his head. "This isn't a good idea."

"Well," Dylan said, "it's what we're doin'."

He grabbed Wakan again, shoving her toward Prichard.

"You and Reilly head back to my cabin," he ordered. "Lock her up good and watch her close."

Prichard took her arm. "What are you gonna do?"

"I'm gonna stay here and watch them drag the Devil's cooked corpse out of the fire. If it takes all night."

Dylan looked around. Some men still tossed bottles into the flames to feed the roar.

***

Time passed in a blur—the sky darkened to deep evening, the cabin reduced to a smoldering skeleton with only a few stubborn fires still burning among the ruins.

Dylan stood staring into the embers, hat in hand to wipe sweat from his brow before replacing it. Cloth wrapped his head, but blood had seeped through, staining it dark around the ruined ear.

Thunder rumbled low in the distance. Dylan glanced up at the heavy clouds rolling in.

Roger Malfry, one of his men, approached cautiously. "Want us to put out what's left of the fire? Start lookin' for his body?"

Dylan shook his head. "Just start digging where the fire's already out. Storm's likely to put it out for us."

Roger nodded and walked off. Hoofbeats thundered closer. Dylan turned as Pete Gentry, the town's lone blacksmith, galloped up and pulled his horse to a skidding stop.

"That Hinderschott feller's callin' for a town meeting this evenin'."

Dylan's jaw tightened. "Probably tryin' to get an early jump for the next election. I ain't too concerned about it."

"That ain't it, Sheriff," Pete said, breathless. "He's tellin' folks that you had the Josephs killed. Says he's got evidence to prove it."

"SHIT!"

Dylan hurled his hat to the ground, all eyes turning to him in the flickering firelight.

"Roger!"

Roger ran over again.

"I want you and Terry to stay here," Dylan barked. "Find that Devil's body and bring it to me the moment you do." He looked around at the other men, all of the waiting for him to give them something to do. "Tell everyone else to mount up. They're comin' with me."

Roger hesitated. "What's goin' on, Sheriff?"

Dylan's eyes burned in the firelight. "It's time I show Elden Hinderschott just who's runnin' this town."

The Knife

THE BACK ROOM OF Sheriff Dylan's cabin was dimly lit. The flame of a single lantern guttered slightly in the draft that slipped through the cracks in the log walls. Prichard and Reilly sat at the rough-hewn table in the center of the room, the Devil's silver pistols placed carefully between them, their etched skulls seeming to watch in silent judgment under the flickering light.

Wakan sat huddled in a small iron cage bolted to the far wall, the bars cold and unforgiving against her back. She watched them quietly, knees drawn up to her chest, eyes wide but defiant in the shadows.

Reilly picked up one of the guns, turning it over in his callused hands. He hooked a finger around the trigger and pulled—nothing. The mechanism refused to budge, as solid and unyielding as stone.

Prichard glanced at him irritably. "Would you stop messin' with it before you blow your head off."

Reilly ignored the warning, eyes narrowed in fascination. "It's the damnedest thing I ever saw. Can't pull the trigger..."

He rotated the pistol slowly, peering at every angle, searching for some hidden catch or lever.

"Can't find any sorta anything to release it." He paused, voice dropping lower. "You reckon those stories are true? Can't nobody but him shoot 'em?"

Prichard stood quickly, chair scraping back against the floorboards. He crossed to the window, parting the threadbare curtains just enough to peer into the black night beyond.

"Done told you," he said, voice edged with frustration. "He weren't nothin' but a man. There's a way to make the guns work. We just gotta figure it out."

Reilly pulled a knife from his belt, the blade glinting briefly, but it was enough to draw Wakan's attention. Reilly began probing carefully behind the trigger guard, trying to pry or wedge something loose.

Wakan's eyes fixed on the knife. It was Lakota—carved bone handle, distinctive pattern etched along the blade, the kind carried by warriors from her village.

"Where did you get that knife?" she asked, voice small but steady, cutting through the quiet.

Reilly's head snapped toward her. "Shut up!"

Prichard turned from the window, glancing first at her, then at Reilly. He saw the knife digging at the trigger mechanism.

"Don't you scratch up my new guns," he warned, voice low and sharp.

Reilly didn't stop, focused intently. "Just...let me figure this out."

Prichard's gaze lingered on Wakan a moment longer.

"How about it, kid?" he asked, stepping closer to the cage. "That Devil tell you how to shoot them guns?"

Wakan stared back at him, unflinching for a heartbeat, then slowly slunk deeper into the corner of the cage, as far from him as the small space allowed.

Phoenix

T HE RUINS OF MAGGIE'S cabin smoldered under the moon- less night sky, the last stubborn flames licking at charred beams and collapsed walls like dying tongues of fire. Heat still radiated from the blackened debris, warping the air above it in shimmering waves. Roger and Terry worked in the flickering glow, their lanterns placed strategically around the wreckage to cast long, uneven shadows across the ash and splintered wood. The acrid stench of scorched flesh clung to their clothes and throats.

Terry shoveled half-heartedly at a pile of rubble, sweat cutting trails through the soot on his face despite the cold.

"This is stupid," he muttered, voice thick with exhaustion and irritation. "I can't see shit out here."

Roger kept his back to him, bent over another section, prying at a collapsed beam with a crowbar.

"Just keep lookin'," he said without turning. "Check over by what's left of the table."

Terry glanced toward the spot Roger indicated—a jagged table leg jutting up from the debris like a broken bone, embers still glowing faintly around it.

"It's still burnin' over there."

"Which means it's a place we ain't checked," Roger replied, voice flat and unyielding. "Now go do it."

Terry shook his head, muttering under his breath as he trudged over. He nudged lighter pieces of debris aside with his boot, then reached for the table leg. His gloved hand closed around it—and he yanked back with a sharp hiss.

"Shit!"

The heat had seeped through the leather. Roger glanced over his shoulder and chuckled low—a dry, humorless sound—before turning away again to focus on his own section.

Terry pulled a rag from his back pocket, wrapped it around the smoldering leg, and heaved. The table slid aside with a scrape of wood on wood, revealing a dark hole beneath the floorboards—jagged edges charred black, smoke still curling lazily from its depths.

Terry leaned over, squinting into the shadows below.

"What's that?"

Roger, still bent over his own pile with his back turned, didn't look up right away. "You say somethin'?"

Behind him, Terry stared down into the hole, brow furrowed.

The weighted blade of the Devil's lasso erupted upward from the darkness in a blur of steel and rope. It punched through Terry's chest with a wet, crunching impact—prongs burying deep between ribs, blood spraying in a hot arc across the rubble. Terry's mouth opened in a silent gasp, eyes bulging as the rope jerked taut. He was yanked downward violently, body folding, boots kicking once against the debris before disappearing into the hole with a muffled thud and a final, gurgling choke.

Roger straightened slowly, crowbar still in hand. "Terry, I didn't hear you. Did you say you found..."

He turned.

The clearing was empty save for the dying flames.

"Terry?"

Silence answered, broken only by the faint crackle of embers.

Slowly, deliberately, the rubble began to shift. The overturned table scraped sideways. Charred floorboards creaked and lifted. Piles of still-burning wood and ash heaved as a figure rose from the hole beneath—tall, coated in soot and blood, eyes burning with cold fury in the lantern light.

Roger stared, mouth slack, fear rooting him to the spot like iron spikes through his boots.

The Devil stood fully upright amid the ruins, rope coiled in one hand, the weighted blade dripping dark and thick onto the ground.

He began spinning it slowly at first, then faster, the prongs whistling through the air in a low, deadly hum.

Roger snapped from his trance, hand fumbling desperately for the pistol at his hip.

But before he could, the sound of the blade sliced through the night.

One Hard Som' Bitch to Kill

P RICHARD PACED THE CREAKING floorboards of Sheriff
Dylan's cabin, boots thudding with restless impatience, his
shadow stretching long and distorted across the walls. Reilly sat
slouched in a chair, idly laying out a game of solitaire, cards slapping down one by one in the heavy quiet. The Lakota knife stuck
upright in the tabletop beside the Devil's cursed guns, its bone
handle gleaming faintly. The keys to the cage were there, too,
glinting whenever the lantern flickered.

Wakan sat curled in the, arms wrapped tight around her knees,
her dark eyes fixed unblinking on the knife—its familiar carvings a
painful reminder in the dim glow.

Prichard stopped pacing abruptly. "How long does it take to
find one dead man in a pile of wood?"

Reilly flipped another card without looking up. "You know the
sheriff. Probably took the body straight into town to show it off to
the town folk."

Prichard strode to a side table cluttered with crumpled wanted posters bearing the Devil's scarred face. He stared down at them, jaw tight, as a flash of lightning outside bleached the room white for an instant, thunder rumbling low and ominous in its wake.

"He should have let me have at 'im," Prichard muttered, voice thick with resentment. "We'd be finished with this by now."

Reilly shrugged, placing a card. "Or it might be your body they're fishin' around for at that cabin."

Prichard whirled, eyes blazing. "Bullshit! That Devil ain't met nobody like me!"

Reilly raised his hands in quick surrender, palms out. "Alright, alright. I meant nothing by it."

Prichard turned back to the posters, breathing hard. After a long moment, he snatched up a thick wad of them and headed for the back door.

Reilly glanced up. "Where you goin'?"

Prichard held up the posters without turning. "To take a shit."

He yanked the door open just as another bolt of lightning split the sky, illuminating the storm-lashed night beyond. Thunder growled like a living thing. He paused in the doorway, rain already spitting in, then looked over at Wakan, his gaze cold and lingering.

"Keepin' her alive was a mistake."

He stormed out, slamming the door hard enough to rattle the lantern. Reilly watched the door a moment, then turned to Wakan with a lazy smirk.

"Well, then. I guess you rub him the wrong way."

Wakan's eyes flicked from Reilly to the knife, then back.

"Where did you get the knife?"

Reilly's smirk faded. "I told you to shut up about it."

"Where did you get the knife?" she repeated, louder this time.

"Shut up!"

"WHERE DID YOU GET THE KNIFE?"

Reilly surged to his feet, chair scraping violently back, and snatched the knife from the table in one fluid motion.

"THIS KNIFE!?!"

He stalked toward the cage, toying with the blade as he walked—flipping it, catching it, running his thumb along the edge until a thin line of blood welled up.

"I took it off another no-good mongrel like you."

He crouched close to the bars, face inches from hers, breath sour with whiskey and tobacco.

"Just after one of our hunters put a bullet in his head. Just like they're gonna do to you tomorrow."

Wakan's eyes blazed. She spat full in his face.

Reilly recoiled, shock flashing across his features, spit dripping down his cheek.

"Why, you little shit!"

He lunged, reaching through the bars with his free hand, fingers clawing for her throat or hair. She twisted away, pressing hard against the back of the cage, but he stretched deeper, snagging the fabric of her dress, yanking her forward.

Lightning flashed again, bleaching the room white.

"Come here!" he snarled. "I'm gonna teach you some manners!"

Another flash—and this time the Devil's shadow loomed huge behind him, silent and sudden.

Wakan's mouth fell open. Reilly sensed it, turned slowly—

A heavy *THWOMP!*—the weighted blade punched through his collarbone with a wet crunch of bone and meat, blood erupting in a hot gush down his chest. Then he was hauled upward, feet kicking wildly, boots scraping the floor before he was lifted clear, neck snapping sideways in the noose. Blood poured from the wound in thick ropes, splattering the table, the cards, the floor in dark, steaming pools.

Wakan gasped, hands over her mouth.

The Devil snatched the cage keys from the table and tossed them to her. She caught them shakily.

"Meet me out front."

He moved to the back door. As Wakan fumbled with the lock:

"Where are you going?"

"I need to take care of Prichard." He opened the door, standing framed against the storm. "If I don't do it now—"

BOOM!

The shotgun blast hit him square in the chest at close range. The impact hurled him backward, his body skidding across the floor that was already slick with Reilly's blood.

Wakan jumped back with a cry, dismay flooding her face.

Prichard stepped slowly into the doorway, shotgun smoking, a grim smile on his face as rain lashed in behind him.

He cracked the chamber open, spent shells clattering to the floor, and calmly reloaded from his shirt pocket.

"My daddy used to tell me," he said, voice steady, "always keep a shotgun in the shitter."

He clicked the chamber shut, resting the barrel on his shoulder, and looked at Wakan.

"Now I guess I know why."

He glanced at the Devil's crumpled form. "You know, I never cared much for the Devil of Black Hills. Always knew he was nothin' more than a man with a gun and a reputation."

His gaze shifted to Reilly's body swaying from the rafter, the weighted blade buried deep in the collarbone, blood still dripping in thick, rhythmic drops to the growing pool below.

"But I do admire his work."

The clanging of keys drew his attention. Wakan's hands shook violently as she tried to fit the key into the lock.

Prichard strode over and snatched them from her grasp.

"Now, now. Won't be havin' that. Sheriff wants you right where you are until tomorrow mornin'."

He paused, studying her terrified face.

"Of course..." He pointed the shotgun at the Devil's body. "If he's here..." He turned back to her. "Then where's everybody who was diggin' him out of that fire?"

He sighed, almost regretful. "Guess I need to head over there. See what's what and who's dead. After that, I'll—"

The Devil coughed—a wet, ragged sound.

Prichard's eyes narrowed curiously. The Devil writhed on the floor, clutching his chest.

Prichard walked over slowly and straddled him, shotgun still casual on his shoulder.

"You are one hard som' bitch to kill."

He bent down, felt the Devil's chest roughly, then ripped the shirt open with a tear of fabric. Beneath, the steel plate gleamed, dented and smeared with blood.

Prichard knocked on it with his knuckles. The Devil grimaced in pain.

"Well, now. That explains a lot." He straightened. "Guess I'll just have to shoot you where there ain't no armor."

He raised the shotgun, aiming point-blank at the Devil's head. The Devil squinted, waiting for the end.

Then Prichard lowered it slightly, eyes flicking to the silver pistols on the table.

"Hey," he said, almost conversational, "I don't suppose you'd tell me how to unlock them triggers."

The Devil grimaced through the pain. "Step one: shove 'em up your ass."

Prichard chuckled, a low, ugly sound.

"Yeah, I didn't think so." He set the shotgun on a nearby shelf, checked his pocket watch in the lantern light, then tucked it away. "Well, I got some time. Guess I'll just beat it out of you. Let's have some fun."

He grabbed the Devil by the collar, hauling him up roughly despite the blood and pain. With a grunt, he hurled him across the room. The Devil crashed into the table, legs snapping under his weight, cards and pistols scattering in a clatter.

Wakan watched, pressed against the cage bars, as one pistol skidded to a stop just out of her reach, the other landing on the far side of the wreckage.

The Devil reached weakly for the nearer gun, fingers scraping wood. Prichard closed in fast, driving a boot into his ribs, then another. He flipped the Devil over and landed a headbutt that split skin and dazed him further.

Prichard whirled him around again and threw him sideways. The Devil slammed into the wall, a side table flying, wanted posters fluttering down like dead leaves to cover him as he struggled to rise.

Wakan strained toward the pistol, fingertips brushing half an inch short, face pressed hard against the cold bars.

The Devil pushed to one knee, fists up as Prichard charged. He blocked a wild swing, took an uppercut that snapped his head back, then crashed into a shelf. The shotgun teetered above him. He snatched it, swinging it around—but Prichard kicked it from his grasp and smashed a fist into his jaw.

The Devil staggered, blood streaming from his mouth, but recovered enough to land a sharp jab to Prichard's nose. Cartilage crunched; blood sprayed. Prichard swung blindly; the Devil blocked, countered with a solid punch to the gut.

Wakan rocked the cage desperately, using her weight to inch it closer, fingers stretching until nails scraped wood.

Prichard stumbled, wiped blood from his face, then roared and charged. He wrapped the Devil up and drove him hard into the floor, the impact rattling the lantern.

He raised for punches—first to the face, splitting lip and brow, blood flecking the boards; second to the ribs, eliciting a wet grunt. The third missed as the Devil twisted; Prichard's fist smashed into the floor, opening up his knuckles.

The Devil kneed him hard in the groin, shoved him off with a surge of desperate strength.

Both men scrambled to their feet, circling, fists raised, breathing ragged. Blood dripped from noses, mouths, brows. The Devil landed a kick to Prichard's knee; Prichard caught the next leg, yanking the Devil off balance and slamming him down again.

"Enough of this!" Prichard snarled.

He snatched the shotgun, racked it, and aimed at the Devil's head. The Devil threw up his hands in a fruitless attempt to cover his face.

BOOM!

Prichard's stomach exploded outward in a wet spray of gore—intestines spilling in ropes, blood and tissue splattering the walls and floor. He stared down in shock, shotgun slipping from numb fingers, then collapsed forward in a heavy, twitching heap atop the Devil.

The Devil rolled the body off, wincing as he did, soaked in fresh blood and viscera. He looked toward the cage.

Wakan held the silver pistol out through the bars, hands trembling, tears streaking her face.

"I remembered the combination."

The Devil approached slowly, taking the gun gently from her.

"You did good, kid."

He reached through the bars, holding one of her hands.

"Real good." He looked around the room. "Keys?"

She nodded toward Prichard's corpse. The Devil searched the bloodied shirt pocket, found them slick with gore, and moved to the cage lock.

"You came back for me," she said.

"I came back for my guns."

"But you left your guns."

"Realized I missed them."

"I saved your life. Again."

"I think I had it under control."

She tilted her head, a faint smile breaking through. He smirked and winked as the lock clicked open.

Wakan rushed out and threw her arms around his neck. The Devil stiffened, arms hovering uncertainly, then slowly wrapped them around her in a careful embrace.

"I shouldn't have left you," he murmured. "I won't do it again."

She nodded against his shoulder, then pulled away.

"Maggie?"

He shook his head slowly. Wakan hung hers, grief fresh.

Then her eyes caught the Lakota knife discarded on the blood-soaked floor. She walked over, bent, and picked it up, fingers tracing the carvings.

"This was my father's knife."

The Devil sighed, voice heavy. "I'm sorry." He paused. "Look. I know you want to get home to your people. But we need to finish th is."

She turned to him.

"For your father. For Maggie."

Wakan looked at him a long moment, then nodded firmly.

Follow the Trail of Bodies

THE NIGHT AIR IN Buffalo Ridge hung cold and heavy, the kind of cold that seeped into a man's bones and made every breath feel sharp. The rain, coming down in sheets now, didn't he lp.

A handful of horses stamped restlessly at the hitching rail outside Skinny's Bar, their flanks steaming in the lantern light spilling from the windows. Two covered wagons sat nearby, canvas flaps tied down against the wind, wheels crusted with frozen mud. A couple of men pushed through the batwing doors, coats pulled tight, spurs jingling as they disappeared inside.

Within, the bar was packed tight—every stool taken, every chair occupied, men standing shoulder to shoulder in the narrow aisles between tables. The reek of sweat and tobacco smoke hung low. Lanterns glinted off hardened, rain-streaked faces and holstered pistols. A low rumble of conversation filled the room.

Elden Hinderschott stood at the front, near the bar, four supporters flanking him—solid men of the town, faces grim and resolute. The crowd watched him with a mix of curiosity and growing unease.

"Gentlemen," Elden began, voice steady but carrying the weight of the hour, "I know it's late, and I wouldn't have asked you to come this evening if it wasn't important."

He held up the folded papers the Devil had given him, raising them high so all could see. "What I have here in my hand is evidence—solid proof—that the sheriff of our town...a man many of you have known all your lives...has been involved in illegal activity."

A ripple of murmurs spread through the room. Heads shook in disbelief. A few men waved him off with dismissive gestures, muttering under their breath.

"His crimes include fraudulent business practices, kidnapping, even murder," Elden pressed on, voice rising slightly. "He's killed people of the Lakota tribe!"

The murmurs grew louder, restless. Men stood in anger. Skinny, behind the bar, folded his arms tight across his chest in clear perturbation.

As voices rose in discontent—ad-libbed shouts of "Bullshit!" and "Sit down, Hinderschott!"—Elden had to raise his voice to be heard over the growing clamor.

"And it's not just the sheriff! It's his deputies—little more than henchmen—who handle all the dirty work! They're the ones who killed Pastor Josephs and his wife! And I also have a long list of people in our community...business people...prosperous people...who...who..."

The crowd erupted then, raucous and angry. More men surged to their feet, some heading for the doors, others shouting Elden d own.

"Wait!" Elden called desperately. "If you'll just hear me out! The evidence is here! You can see it for yourself!"

Slow, deliberate clapping echoed from the back room. The sound cut through the noise like a knife. Dylan emerged, clapping steadily as he walked forward, a host of his men filing in behind him—hard-eyed deputies and armed supporters, filling the space with menace. Dylan's bandages around his ear were soaked darker now, fresh blood seeping through the cloth.

"That's great, Mister Hinderschott!" Dylan said, voice booming with mock admiration. "Real fine. Some of the best story-telling I've heard since Skinny over there got drunk and told us about that time his wife was tendin' their pigs and he walked by and said...what was that you said, Skinny?"

Skinny shifted uncomfortably behind the bar. "I says, 'I wonder when we got that new pig.'"

Laughter rolled through Dylan's men, sharp and forced. The rest of the crowd chuckled uneasily, tension thick.

"That's right," Dylan continued, grinning wide. "That didn't go over so well, did it, Skinny?"

Skinny shook his head, forcing a weak smile as more laughter rippled.

"No, it didn't."

Dylan's grin faded as he turned fully to Elden.

"So, Mister Hinderschott, this evidence you claim to have on me...where'd you say you got it?"

Elden stared at him a long moment, the papers trembling slightly in his grip. "The Devil..." he mumbled.

"What's that?" Dylan cupped a hand to his good ear. "Speak up so we can all hear you."

Elden swallowed hard. "The Devil of Black Hills gave it—"

"The Devil of Black Hills gave it to you."

Dylan nodded slowly, letting the words sink in. Gasps and mutters spread like wildfire through the room.

"The most ruthless, murderin' piece of scum..." Dylan continued, voice dripping contempt, "the man everyone in town's been after, gave you evidence that I committed all kinds of crimes and, what? You just believed him?"

Elden held the papers higher. "It's written in Paul Josephs' hand."

Dylan tilted his head. "And you know this how? You have other samples of his handwriting? 'Cause I'd think most of that would have burned up with his cabin."

Elden faltered, shaken, grasping for words.

"Surely...there's probably something in my store's books...if I were to go through my records..."

"Uh-huh." Dylan's tone was mocking. "Of course. A bigger question is, what's your relationship with this murderin' Devil? Are the two of you in some kind of cahoots?"

Elden shook his head vehemently. "Of course not."

"Why didn't you sound the alarm and tell everyone he was here? Are you protecting him?"

The room grew quieter, the weight of accusation settling heavy. Elden opened his mouth, but no words came.

Dylan's gaze swept the crowd. "And you mentioned somethin' about the Lakota tribe. Some kinda crimes committed against them? Let me ask you this: Do you really think anyone here cares?"

Heads shook. Murmurs of agreement rose.

"Do you think anyone in this town would lose sleep if a few of those savages were killed? Hell, if their whole damn tribe were wiped out for that matter?"

Nods and vocal support rippled through the room—"That's right!" "Damn straight!" "They're in the way!"

Dylan pulled back his coat, revealing his sidearm, hand resting easy on the butt.

"Now, that Devil is dead. There's a pine box in front of my sheriff's office, and my men will be puttin' his body in it for all to see." He paused, letting it sink in. "But I think the Devil's gonna need some company."

His grip tightened on the gun. Behind him, his men mirrored the motion—hands on holsters, rifles lifting slightly. The room shifted as people moved aside, clearing space, the air crackling with sudden menace.

Elden raised a hand in placation, his supporters doing the same.

Skinny edged farther down the bar, putting distance between himself and Elden, positioning near the front window.

Dylan's fingers curled around the grip.

Skinny glanced casually out the window, then did a sharp dou-
ble-take.

"Looks like there's a body already in the box, Sheriff."

Dylan's head snapped toward him, then back to Elden.

"What are you talkin' about?"

Skinny pointed out the window, voice steady but laced with
something darker. "Well, look."

***

Dylan pushed the batwing doors open slowly, peering out into the
shadowed square, the lantern on the sheriff's porch casting a weak,
flickering glow over the pine coffin propped there against one of
the porch posts. Nearly everyone crowded behind him—shoulders
bumping, breaths held—craning necks to see, or pressing to the
windows for a better view.

Dylan stepped down the porch steps with deliberate caution,
boots thudding heavy on the frozen boards. The entire bar emptied behind him in a tense rush, a wave of men spilling into the
street. Elden stayed closest, just a step off Dylan's shoulder, his face
pale but resolute.

They crossed the muddy street in a tight knot, the coffin growing closer.

At the pine box, Dylan and Elden stood side by side, staring up
into the shadowed box.

Just then, lightning forked across the black sky, illuminating the
scene in stark white for a frozen instant, followed by a roll of thun-

der that rattled windows up and down the square. Reilly's corpse lay inside the coffin—grotesque, throat slashed nearly to the spine in a ragged, gaping wound that had soaked his shirtfront black with blood. His head lolled at an unnatural angle, barely attached, tongue protruding swollen and purple from his slack mouth, eyes staring vacant and milky at the stormy sky. Flies already crawled across the congealed mess of flesh and cartilage.

Gasps rippled through the crowd, low moans of horror. Men recoiled, some turning away, hands to mouths. Dylan's face drained of color, going stark white beneath the bloodied bandages around his ear.

He began backing up slowly, eyes darting wildly into every shadow, every alley mouth, every darkened window.

"He's here."

His hand flashed to his holster, drawing his pistol in a blur. Dozens of henchmen followed suit—metal scraping leather, hammers cocking in a staccato chorus that echoed down the street.

"Dammit, he's here!" Dylan screamed.

Elden and his supporters edged sideways, away from the tightening circle of armed men. One of Elden's friends started to draw his own gun, mirroring the others, but Elden clamped a firm hand on his arm and shook his head sharply.

"This ain't our fight."

Dylan stumbled backward into the center of the street, nearly tripping over a loose rock. He shoved a nearby man roughly to the right.

"Spread out! Spread out, dammit! Look sharp!"

The men fanned apart, boots scraping dirt, rifles raised, eyes scanning rooftops and doorways in frantic sweeps.

Then in one of the black windows sheriff's office, one of the men caught sight of a silhouette—a tall figure in a cowboy hat, standing motionless just beyond the glass.

"THERE!" the man yelled.

Dylan's pistol barked wildly, muzzle flashes strobing the night. Every henchman opened fire in a deafening roar—glass exploding inward, the door splintering off its hinges in a hail of lead, wood chips and plaster flying in clouds. The silhouette jerked and danced under the onslaught,. Inside, a latern shattered, lighting the office with a spray of fire.

The fire revealed the figure to be the crude wooden carving of Dylan himself, now bullet-riddled.

"Hold your fire! Hold your fire!" Dylan screamed over the dying echoes. "It's not him!"

The men stood frozen, chests heaving, smoke curling from hot barrels. Tension coiled like a spring, every shadow suddenly alive with threat.

Dylan's eyes darted, catching on a covered wagon parked a few doors down. A thick rope trailed from its rear axle, snaking loose across the street, barely visible in the dirt and gloom.

His gaze followed it—across the muddy ruts, slack and ominous, to where the weighted blade end was wrapped tight around a hitching post on the opposite side.

Realization hit him like ice water.

"Get out of the str—"

A sharp smack echoed from the wagon's rear. The hitched horse bolted forward in panic, wagon lurching into motion at a fast clip.

The rope whipped across the street, snapping taut at knee height. Men toppled like pins—legs swept out from under them, bodies crashing hard into the dirt with grunts and cries. Some tried to jump; most failed, skulls cracking against frozen ground, bones snapping audibly.

As the chaos erupted, the Devil stepped calmly from where the wagon had been parked, pistols blazing. Bullets found falling men mid-tumble—chests erupting in red sprays, throats torn open in wet gouts, faces disintegrating in fountains of blood and bone. One man's knee shattered sideways; he screamed as he hit the ground, only to take a round through the eye that burst the socket in a jelly-like spurt.

Some henchmen scrambled to aim rifles, but the sweeping rope caught them first, sending them sprawling. The Devil walked forward unhurried, firing into backs and exposed necks—spines exploding outward in crimson fans, skulls splitting with wet crunches as brains spilled onto the dirt.

When one pistol clicked empty, he flicked the cylinder release mid-stride; it dropped, clattering to the ground. But before it even hit dirt, his gun hand slapped against his ammo belt, snatching a loaded cylinder and slamming it home with a sharp spin, already firing again before the empty one landed.

The second gun emptied; the same fluid motion—release, slap, lock, fire.

Two men tried to flank around the careening wagon for a clear shot. The horse and wagon thundered over them—hooves pounding flesh to pulp, wheels crushing ribs with sickening cracks, blood and viscera bursting beneath the iron rims.

By the time the wagon rattled to a halt against a hitching rail on the far side, over a dozen bodies lay strewn across the street—limbs twisted at wrong angles, faces frozen in shock, pools of blood spreading thick and glossy under the lantern light, steam rising faintly in the cold.

The Devil stepped into the open street, pistols smoking, walking forward with deliberate calm. Wakan appeared from the shadows near the stopped wagon, detaching the lasso and winding the rope quickly around her arm.

Two men spotted her, swinging rifles toward the child. The Devil's pistols barked twice each, and their heads snapped back, painting gore in wet arcs against storefront walls.

Wakan yanked the weighted blade free from the hitching post, spun it once overhead, and called out. "Hey!"

She flung it toward him. He holstered one gun mid-stride and caught the rope cleanly, grinning faintly as Wakan darted into a nearby doorway.

One man fired desperately. The Devil whipped the blade in a tight circle; it sliced clean through the shooter's neck in a fountain of arterial blood, head toppling to the dirt with a wet thud, body standing a moment longer before collapsing in a twitching heap.

Another henchman fell to a chest shot, ribs and lung tissue exploding outward.

A shot whined from above, splintering wood near the Devil's head. Without looking up, he raised a pistol and fired—once. The rooftop shooter jerked, blood blooming across his shirt, and tumbled forward, crashing through a saloon awning before hitting the street with a bone-crunching impact.

The Devil released the blade again; it thudded into a fleeing man's back, burying deep between shoulder blades with a crunch of spine. The man screamed, staggering forward before dropping face-first into the mud, blood bubbling from his mouth.

Drawing both pistols now, the Devil advanced down the center of the street—firing, slaughtering, reloading with that impossible speed. Bodies dropped in his wake: a man's jaw shattered; another took three rounds to the gut, intestines spilling in wet coils as he crumpled; a third clutched his throat uselessly as blood shot from between his fingers.

Not every bullet aimed at the Devil missed. One henchman slipped around a corner behind him and fired point-blank into his back. The Devil jerked forward, the steel plate beneath his shirt taking the impact with a dull clang, but the force staggered him.

"I got 'im!" the man shouted triumphantly. "I got 'im, but he ain't fallin'!"

Another henchman connected, even closer. The round bounced solidly off the armored plate with a sharp ring, ricocheting into the night. The Devil turned without breaking pace and put two bullets into the man beside him: one through the throat, severing windpipe in a bubbling gush of blood; the second through the eye, socket exploding in a wet spray. The body dropped like a sack, convulsing once before going still.

"He cain't be kilt!" the second shooter screamed, voice high with panic. "The stories are true! He cain't be kilt!"

The words spread like wildfire. Henchmen faltered, rifles lowering, faces twisting in horror as they stared at the advancing figure—bloodied, scarred, unstoppable. One by one, they broke: turning, running, boots pounding the dirt as they fled into alleys and side streets, some firing blindly over their shoulders, bullets whining harmlessly into the night.

Elden and his crew watched from the sidelines, pressed against the storefronts, mouths agape as the retreat turned to rout.

"Get back here!" Dylan bellowed, voice cracking with fury and fear.

He aimed at the Devil again—click. Empty.

Panic seized him. He fumbled desperately in his pocket for bullets, fingers slick with sweat and blood, holding the pistol tight against his chest as rounds clattered loose to the ground.

"Where are you goin'?" he screamed again at the fleeing men.

Time slowed, the world narrowing to the Devil's advance. Anger burned cold in his eyes, fearlessness etched in every deliberate step. Behind him, the sheriff's office blazed—a roaring inferno that silhouetted him in hellish orange and crimson, flames licking the sky like the fires of damnation itself. Shadows danced across his scarred face, the noose mark around his neck stark in the firelight, turning him into something primordial, something that struck terror straight to the bone. He may very well have been the devil himself, risen from the pit to claim what was owed.

He fired again—dropping another body mid-flight. He extended both arms, firing blind into the scattering crowd, killing two more with precise, merciless shots: one through the spine, paralyzing him in a twitching heap; the other through the base of the skull, brain matter erupting in a grisly halo.

More henchmen threw down weapons and ran, trampling each other in their haste, screams echoing down the street as the Devil reloaded on the move—cylinder dropping, new one slapping home, firing resuming without pause.

Dylan's hands shook violently as he scooped bullets from the dirt, mud caking his fingers. A shot took him in the shoulder—flesh tearing open in a ragged bloom, blood jetting hot and thick down his arm. He screamed, staggering.

Dylan backed away, terror naked in his eyes, firing wildly. A henchman beside him took a round to the temple.

Dylan gritted his teeth, retreating step by step.

Another bullet caught Dylan in the shoulder. He screamed, blood soaking his coat instantly.

"Elden! Elden, do something!"

Elden and his men watched from the sidelines, hands frozen away from their guns.

Another round tore into Dylan's leg, meat and bone shredding as once. He howled, collapsing to one knee, then crawling backward through the mud, leaving a smeared crimson trail.

"Kill him, Elden! Kill him!"

Elden shook his head slowly, eyes wide.

Dylan fumbled a single bullet into his cylinder with shaking, blood-slick fingers. He raised the gun—but a shot shattered his arm at the elbow, bone splintering outward in white shards wrapped in red meat. The pistol spun away. Dylan screamed again, dragging himself on his belly now, one good arm clawing at the dirt.

"Elden! Please! Throw me a gun!"

Elden's hand hovered near his holster, but the Devil's cold glance pinned it there. Elden let it drop.

The Devil fired once more—a round slamming into the small of Dylan's back, spine shattering with a wet crack. Dylan's final scream cut off in a gurgling choke as he collapsed face-down in the mud.

The Devil stood over him, smoke curling from both barrels. Dylan rolled weakly onto his back, bloodied and broken, defiance burning in his eyes even now.

"Do you expect me to beg for mercy!?!"

The Devil raised a pistol, barrel steady on Dylan's forehead.

"Mercy ain't really what I'm known for."

The shot rang out. Dylan's head snapped back, a neat red hole appearing center-forehead, the back of his skull bursting outward, splattering the dirt behind him. His body slumped.

Silence fell, broken only by the crackle of flames from the sheriff's office and the low moan of wind through the square.

The Devil held both guns out, fingers moving along the grips. Buttons slid back in with soft clicks, locking the triggers once more.

Townspeople began emerging cautiously from buildings—doors creaking open, faces pale in upper windows, staring at the carnage: bodies twisted and torn, blood pooling thick and steaming in the cold, the street a slaughter pen under the flickering lanterns.

Elden and his men couldn't move.

Wakan stepped from the shadows, walking toward the Devil. He looked at her and nodded once. She nodded back.

Then she snickered softly.

"What?"

Doing her best gravelly impression: "Mercy ain't really what I'm known for."

Elden watched the exchange, stunned.

"You didn't like that?" the Devil asked.

She shrugged. "Kinda silly."

The Devil scratched his forehead with the barrel of one gun. "Well, it's not like I rehearsed it. I think in the spur of the moment—"

BANG!

A shot cracked from an alley. The Devil jerked, blood blooming high on his upper arm as he dropped to the ground.

Everyone jumped, heads whipping toward the sound.

Prichard limped from the shadows behind Wakan, pistol raised. A bloody blanket was wrapped tight around his midsection, soaked dark—probably the only thing holding in his guts. His face was gray with pain and blood loss, but his eyes burned.

He shoved Wakan roughly toward the Devil. She stumbled to his side.

Elden and his men reached for weapons, but Prichard swung his pistol toward Wakan's head.

"Don't! I'll kill her!"

The Devil pushed to his knees, clutching his bleeding arm, then reached slowly for a gun. Prichard cocked his hammer, pressing the barrel to Wakan's temple.

"You do anything with those guns other than toss them to me, I'll put her down."

The Devil met Wakan's eyes. She shook her head faintly.

Slowly, using thumb and forefinger, the Devil drew both pistols and tossed them into the dirt at Prichard's feet.

Prichard kept the gun on Wakan, bending painfully to snatch one up with his free hand, blood dripping steadily from beneath the blanket.

"I ain't got long to live," he rasped. "This little bitch saw to that. But I plan on takin' you with me, Devil."

He examined the silver pistol, tried the trigger—locked.

"But first, you're gonna tell me how to unlock the triggers."

The Devil grimaced through the pain in his arm. "The hell I will. You ain't killin' me with my own gun."

"Tell me now, or I'll kill her!"

"GO TO HELL!"

Prichard pistol-whipped Wakan across the temple. She crumpled hard to the dirt, dazed.

"OKAY!" the Devil yelled.

Prichard's eyes locked on him.

"I'll tell you," the Devil said, voice strained, "but you have to promise not to hurt her."

"No, don't!" Wakan mumbled from the ground.

"Promise me!"

Prichard sneered. "I promise you I'll kill her now if you don't!"

The Devil closed his eyes, head lowering in defeat.

"On the back of the grip," he said quietly, "there's a metal slide. Push it in."

Prichard kept the gun on Wakan and fumbled with the pistol. The buttons slid out.

"What's next?"

Elden stepped forward. "Prichard, you don't have to do this. We can get the doctor. We can still—"

"Shut up, Elden. What's next?"

The Devil met Elden's eyes briefly, then looked to the ground.

"Press them in the order I tell you. Top two."

Prichard pressed the top two.

"Bottom two."

He pressed those.

"Top and bottom."

He pressed those.

"Top three."

Wakan, struggling to her knees, cut her eyes to the Devil. Their gazes locked—she knew that wasn't right.

Prichard pressed the top three buttons. A soft click sounded. He grinned through blood-flecked teeth.

He raised the pistol toward the Devil—but it wasn't the Devil's gun in his other hand.

"Oh, I plan on killin' you with your own gun," he said, voice dripping venom. "But first you're gonna watch me kill her with it
."

He leveled the silver revolver at Wakan's head.

Elden drew his pistol. "Put the gun down, Prichard."

Prichard's aim stayed steady on Wakan. Elden's men drew theirs.

"We'll cut you down the moment you pull the trigger!" Elden warned.

"I'm already dead!"

Prichard's finger tightened, smile widening as he stared at the Devil. Then he pulled the trigger.

BOOM!

The pistol exploded in a blinding flash and thunderous roar. Prichard's hand disintegrated. Bone shards, fingers, and shredded meat flew in all directions. His palm was torn to ruin.

Prichard screamed, staggering back, clutching the mangled stump as blood jetted in thick pulses.

The Devil rose calmly, dusting off his hat and placing it on his head. He reached down and retrieved his second pistol from the dirt.

He looked at Wakan, surprise on her face amid the ringing silence.

"One combination unlocks the trigger," he told her quietly. "But another one blocks the barrel."

Wakan smiled through the shock.

The Devil moved his fingers swiftly along the grip of his gun, then aimed at Prichard—who knelt in the dirt, cradling his ruined hand. He had released the blanket, which had, in turn, released his innards.

Prichard looked up, face twisted in agony and hate.

"I'll see you in hell."

"Keep it warm for me."

The shot took Prichard in the forehead. His body toppled forward, landing atop Dylan's corpse in a heap.

The Devil holstered his gun, then gently touched the side of Wakan's head where Prichard had struck her.

"You okay?"

She nodded, then snickered again despite everything.

He sighed.

"You know, there just ain't no pleasin' you." He paused, then added softly, "Would you go fetch our horse, could you do that much?"

Smiling through the tears and blood, Wakan scampered off.

The Devil watched her go with a faint smirk, shaking his head. He bent over the bodies, shoving Prichard's corpse aside, then pulled Dylan's lapel open and ripped the sheriff's badge free with a sharp tug.

Guns cocked behind him—sharp, metallic clicks cutting the silence.

He glanced over his shoulder. Elden and three colleagues stood with pistols aimed at his back.

"Mister," Elden said, voice steady but edged with steel, "I don't know who you are. But I can speak to the things you're accused of doing."

The Devil stood slowly, back still to them, badge glinting in his blood-slick fingers.

"You've terrorized this community and many more like it across this country for long enough."

The Devil turned gradually, hand hovering near but not touching his holstered gun.

"As a citizen of Buffalo Ridge," Elden continued, "it is my sworn duty..."

Three pistols clattered into the dirt at Elden's feet.

"...to place you..."

Elden glanced down, then to his sides—his men backing away slowly, hands raised in surrender.

"...under citizen's..."

He sighed, holstering his own gun.

The Devil nodded once and strode toward Elden. Elden straightened, chin lifted, attempting stoic fearlessness as the figure approached.

The Devil slapped the sheriff's badge into Elden's chest. Elden caught it reflexively.

"This town's gonna need a new sheriff," the Devil said quietly. "I figure you'll do."

He started to turn.

"Yeah?" Elden called after him. "Well, I'm sorry but it doesn't work like that."

The Devil faced him again.

"Our sheriffs are chosen by the will of the people through a free and fair election."

The Devil nodded, then looked around at the townsfolk emerging from doorways and windows—faces pale, eyes wide with awe and lingering terror.

"Anybody got a problem with this man here bein' sheriff?"

No one spoke. They were too afraid to.

"Seems unanimous."

He turned away once more, moving toward Wakan leading their horse.

Elden followed a step. "Even so, I'm the last person you want to see as sheriff. Because I'll be coming after you. I'll hunt you down and see that justice is served for the things you've done! I'll make sure you hang!"

The Devil pulled his collar away, revealing the thick, puckered scar circling his neck.

"People tried that. Didn't take."

"You think I'm kidding?" Elden's voice rose. "I'll tack up your wanted poster in every town from here to the Mississippi. Every lawman and bounty hunter will be gunnin' for you. This time, there won't be any place you can hide!"

The Devil spun suddenly, eyes blazing.

"I AIN'T HIDIN'!"

Elden stumbled back a step.

"I've been hidin' now for fifteen years," the Devil said, voice low and raw, "but there ain't no use in it. Because no matter how far I run...no matter how deep I bury my head in the sand...I always end up here."

He spread his arms, taking in the carnage—the bodies strewn like broken toys, blood soaking the dirt in dark lakes, the sheriff's office burning steadily behind him, flames painting his silhouette in hellish orange.

"Right. Back. Here!"

Wakan walked the horse up beside him. He reached for the reins.

"So you wanna send people after me, go ahead. You wanna tell the world I'm alive, you do that. I'll be easy to find."

He mounted swiftly behind her, settling into the saddle.

"Just follow the trail of bodies."

Wakan whipped the reins, and they galloped away into the night, hooves thundering down the street and out of town, leaving only dust, blood, and silence in their wake.

Epilogue: The Souls of Man

THE MOON HUNG LOW over the ruins of the Josephs' cabin. The Devil sat astride his horse near the barn, reins loose in his hand, gaze fixed on the dark doorway where Wakan had disappeared moments earlier. The night air carried the faint, lingering smell of old smoke from the long-cold ashes of the burned house. He waited in silence, the horse shifting occasionally beneath him, breath steaming in the chill.

Eventually, the barn door creaked open. Wakan emerged, leading Ithánčhan by a gentle hand on the mare's neck. The horse followed willingly, no saddle upon its back, no reins or bridle—just the trust between girl and beast.

The Devil watched her approach, a faint smile tugging at the corner of his scarred mouth. "That's one pretty horse," he said quietly. "But how you gonna ride 'er without a saddle?"

Wakan looked up at him, eyes bright in the moonlight. "Well..."

***

In the side field, the dark expanse stretched wide and empty under the moon's cold glow, the forest a black wall in the distance. Itháņčhan galloped, mane flying, hooves thundering, free toward the horizon. The mare's silhouette grew smaller and smaller, until she vanished into the night, reclaiming the wild she had been born to

The Devil and Wakan stood side by side at the field's edge, watching the horse disappear. He reached out slowly and placed an arm around her narrow shoulders, drawing her close. She leaned into him, and they both smiled—quiet, shared, bittersweet. Tears glistened on Wakan's cheeks in the moonlight.

"Come on," he said, voice rough with something gentle. "Let's get you home."

***

The journey unfolded in quiet, steady moments across the changing land.

They rode down a narrow trail as the sun first peeked over the distant trees, its early rays painting the frost-kissed grass in pale gold, the horse's breath and theirs mingling in the crisp dawn air.

They traversed a shallow creek, guiding the horse slowly across the clear, cold water that rushed around its legs, splashing softly, the reflection of the sky rippling on the surface.

Deep in the woods, the Devil walked ahead, leading the horse by the reins while Wakan lay draped across its neck, asleep, her small body rising and falling gently with the animal's steady gait, the forest quiet around them save for birdsong and the rustle of leaves.

The sun slid behind towering mountains as they trotted toward them, the peaks turning deep purple and orange in the fading light, long shadows stretching across the trail.

Morning came again, bright and clear. They crested a high hill, pausing at the top. In the valley below spread Wakan's Lakota reservation—dozens of tipis dotted the landscape like pale cones against the earth, smoke rising thin and straight from campfires where figures moved about in the early light, tending horses, carrying water, beginning the day's quiet rhythms.

They rode down into the reservation, the Devil and Wakan drawing curious stares. Lakota men, women, and children paused in their tasks—mending hides, stirring pots, leading ponies—to watch the odd pair pass through, whispers following in their wake.

A Lakota chief—tall, weathered, his presence calm and commanding—stood waiting ahead. Wakan pulled the horse to a gentle stop beside him.

"There you are, Wakan," the chief said, voice deep and warm. "Your mother will be pleased you're safe."

He looked up at the Devil, who met his gaze and nodded once in quiet respect.

"You best not keep her waitin'," the Devil said calmly to Wakan.

Wakan turned suddenly and threw her arms around his neck in a fierce hug. This time, he didn't hesitate—his arms wrapped around her small frame, holding her close, one hand resting gently on her back.

When she pulled away, eyes shining, she asked, "Will I see you again?"

He shook his head slowly. "Can't say. But if I come through these parts again, I'll be sure to find you."

She hung her head. He lifted her chin with a careful finger.

"Hey."

She looked up at him, tears brimming. He leaned close and whispered in her ear, words meant only for her.

When he drew back, she looked at him curiously.

"That's my name," he said. "My real name."

She smiled wider.

"Now, don't you go tellin' the world."

"I won't."

With the chief's steady help, she climbed down from the horse. She turned and waved once, then hurried toward the village.

A Lakota woman emerged from a nearby tipi, pausing at the entrance. She saw Wakan and pressed a hand to her mouth in disbelief and joy.

"Ina!" Wakan cried, running to her.

The woman—her mother—scooped her up in a crushing embrace, holding her daughter tight as tears fell freely.

The Devil and the chief watched the reunion in silence.

"You know," the chief said after a moment, "our Medicine Woman..."

He nodded toward a beautifully adorned older Lakota woman, who peeked cautiously from the door of a nearby tipi, her eyes sharp and knowing.

"...foretold of your coming. She's dreamed of late of a great darkness, bringing with it misery that will swallow the souls of man."

The Devil raised his eyebrows slightly.

"Our chieftains wanted to greet you with a hundred of our best warriors bearing spears."

The Devil glanced around—no warriors, no spears in sight.

"So, I guess your Medicine Woman changed her mind about me."

The chief shook his head. "No. She said that no weapon could pierce your flesh, and that we would only anger you, and then you would slaughter us all."

The Devil raised his eyebrows again, higher this time.

"Well...I guess a bad reputation is better than no reputation at all."

He smiled faintly. The chief shrugged.

"There's some men been killin' your people," the Devil said. "Now, most of 'em are dead...but some of 'em's still breathin'. If you speak to the new sheriff over in Buffalo Ridge, you might get their names out of 'im."

"And why would I do that?"

The Devil shrugged. "Retribution."

The chief stared at him a moment. "That's not really our way."

The Devil stared down at him, studying him. "Suit yourself," he said finally.

He started to turn the horse. The chief noticed the fresh blood soaking through the Devil's sleeve where the bullet had pierced his arm.

"You're wounded."

The Devil glanced at it. "Yeah. Hey, I don't suppose your Medicine Woman would dress it for me properly, would she?"

The chief looked back at the old woman. The concern on her face was telling.

"Probably not a good idea. If she sees you can bleed, she might rethink the effectiveness of our spears."

The Devil nodded. "Good point."

He started to turn the horse again.

"Where will you go?"

The Devil looked at the wound. "For this? I've had worse."

He reached into his saddlebag and pulled out his mangled, cursed sidearm, the metal twisted grotesquely.

"I've gotta see a man about a gun."

The chief regarded the ruined pistol cautiously, then nodded.

The Devil turned the horse fully, and the Lakota tribe gathered quietly to watch him ride away—men, women, children standing in silent clusters, eyes following the scarred man until he vanished into the trees.

THE END

About the Author

Little is known about Joseph Xand. What is known are the things of myth. He wanted to be a famous writer, mostly of horror novels, although his interests ranged into science fiction, young adult, westerns, and more. He struggled to make a living at it.□

In the early 1980s, Joseph Xand packed up a few things, including his typewriter, and headed off into the wilderness of Southeast Oklahoma on a spiritual journey to find himself. □

He was never seen again.□

Occasionally, his writings emerge from the ether (sometimes handwritten, sometimes typed), and we do what we can to polish and publish them.□

The locals sometimes refer to that area of Oklahoma where he disappeared as Xandland.

www.ingramcontent.com/pod-product-compliance
Lightning Source LLC
Chambersburg PA
CBHW070931250626

47159CB00009B/3202